"Paula, what's wrong?"

Ben's voice was husky as he cradled her against his hard body. "Are you nervous about what's happening between us?"

"Maybe a little," she conceded. His proximity was doing insidious things to her senses. "I'm not really sure what *is* happening . . . between us."

"Attraction," he murmured. "And it's powerful stuff." His hand moved deliberately over her hip, stoking a fire deep within her. "So why fight it?"

Jane Silverwood used to teach college English. But after grading nearly ten thousand compositions, she decided to strike out on her own. She wrote numerous magazine articles before turning to romance writing and now truly enjoys sitting down at her computer each day with the characters and situations she left the night before. In her spare time Jane skates, sails and "collects" Chinese restaurants.

Books by Jane Silverwood

HARLEQUIN TEMPTATION

These books may be available at your local bookseller.

Don't miss any of our special offers. Write to us at the following address for information on our newest releases.

Harlequin Reader Service
901 Fuhrmann Blvd., P.O. Box 1397, Buffalo, NY 14240
Canadian address: P.O. Box 603,
Fort Erie, Ont. L2A 9Z9

A Permanent Arrangement

JANE SILVERWOOD

Harlequin Books

TORONTO • NEW YORK • LONDON
AMSTERDAM • PARIS • SYDNEY • HAMBURG
STOCKHOLM • ATHENS • TOKYO • MILAN

Published August 1986

ISBN 0-373-25217-X

Printed in Canada

1

AT SEVEN IN THE MORNING of what promised to be another sweltering day, the small shopping center near Paula Kirk's home was deserted. Yesterday afternoon the temperature had hit one hundred, and today the prediction was for the mercury to shoot even higher. Maryland in July, she mused, glancing at the tightly closed storefronts.

The pet shop where her son, Nat, had liked to purchase his tropical fish was still boarded up, but there were indications that it was being refurbished. The old Going Out of Business sign was gone, and a fresh coat of paint had recently been applied to the exterior. Was the place still going to be a pet shop, she wondered. And if so, what brave soul was going to take a shot at making it pay for itself?

Next door, the hairdresser had a window filled with grooming aids and pictures of smoothly coiffed models. As Paula passed it on the way to the convenience store, which was the only business open at this time of the morning, she ran a self-conscious hand through her long, straight hair. She had it tied up in a careless ponytail, but when it hung loose it reached the middle of her back. Since her teen years, Paula's thick, pale gold locks had been her pride. But her thirty-first birthday was coming up in a couple of weeks. The evening before, as she'd given her tresses their nightly one hundred brush strokes, she'd asked herself if it wasn't time to have them cut short.

A quarter of an hour later, Paula was still mulling this question over. Carrying two boxes of Nat's favorite cereal, she emerged from the path onto a side street and made her way along the route that led back to Parcel Court, where she lived. Other than the rhythmic thud of her feet on the concrete, the only sounds punctuating the stillness were the hum of air conditioners and the eerie drone of cicadas.

It was still many minutes before eight o'clock, so she didn't expect to run into anybody. But as she approached her corner, she caught sight of a tall, lean figure pushing a hand mower along the strip of turf by the sidewalk. Paula cocked her head. Apparently the new man on the street had an unconventional turn of mind. It had never occurred to her to cut her own grass in the cool of the early morning, but she supposed it made sense.

Hoisting her grocery bag a little higher, Paula strode forward at her usual brisk clip. This was a good opportunity to introduce herself, she decided. Parcel Court was a settled street of mostly older couples who, with one notable exception, kept to themselves. Nevertheless, all its residents were acquainted, got together for an annual Labor Day picnic and usually had a friendly word or two when they encountered one another at the mailbox. But the ranch house on the corner was a rental. People in it came and went every few months, so it wasn't always easy to keep track of who was living there, and a woman as busy as Paula didn't really feel like regularly rushing over with a plate of fresh-baked cookies just to find out.

Between her hectic schedule and the heat, which had been keeping everyone inside, Paula hadn't even noticed this new tenant until four days ago. When she'd caught sight of him disappearing into his garage, she'd had to admit that he certainly stood out from the others. For one thing, unlike the majority of suburban husbands one saw puttering in their yards, there was not an extra ounce of fat on his muscular frame. He didn't, she'd thought with a whimsical smile, look married—though of course he must be. Otherwise what was he doing renting a big house with a yard full of grass to mow?

On one occasion since then, she'd passed him while running on the path in the woods. Something about his long-legged stride and thatch of iron-gray hair had made her think of a wolf. The impression had been intensified by her brief glimpse of his face. On his ruggedly masculine countenance, there were lines from his nose to his mouth that suggested he was a man who'd been around and hadn't always liked what he'd seen. She'd guessed that he was somewhere in his late thirties or early forties, and she'd thought him good-looking, but not in the conventional way.

Indeed, she'd sensed right away that there was nothing conventional about him. In that fleeting instant when she'd glanced up as he passed and seen his cool blue eyes focus on her and warm with interest, little prickles of sensation had danced on her skin, and she'd immediately decided to give him a wide berth. But that was silly, she now told herself sternly. You didn't refuse to be civil to a new neighbor who lived across the street from you just because he was good-looking.

As she approached the corner the object of her attention looked up. Spying her, he gave the lawn mower one last cursory shove and then rested his hands on his hips and waited.

"Hi, there." His voice was a pleasant baritone, well modulated and resonant, but not as striking as her husband Tim's had been. Before his illness Tim had been the anchorman on a Washington, D.C., news show.

"Hello." Paula smiled and slowed her pace.

He answered her smile with one of his own. "I haven't had a chance to introduce myself. I believe we're neighbors."

"It certainly looks that way." Stopping, she turned toward him and nodded pleasantly.

"You live in the white colonial with the green shutters, don't you?"

Mutely she nodded again and struggled not to scrutinize him too openly. Though there was nothing unusual about a summer tan, this man must have spent a great deal of time in the sun. Below the brief corduroy shorts that hugged narrow hips, his long legs were deep brown and sinewy. They were a match for his arms and his graceful, long-fingered hands. Encasing the well-defined muscles of his chest and shoulders was a ragged red T-shirt with the legend, Beer Lover, topping a picture of a foamy glass. On him, the T-shirt was inexplicably attractive.

"I even know your name. It's Kirk, isn't it? Paula Kirk?"

Now she did stare. "How did you—"

"I'm an ex-spy." He grinned, and as his ice-blue eyes crinkled at the corners, his whole expression was changed, the hard edges that defined the character of his face visibly softening. His voice, as he continued his explanation, was boyishly conspiratorial. "The lady up the street told me. I'm sure you know the one. I've repressed her name, but I remember distinctly that her hair looks like cotton candy."

Paula's eyebrows shot up and she choked back a gurgling laugh. "Bernadette?"

"That's her, and a very well-informed female she is. She jumped out at me when I went to get the mail and gave me a briefing on my new neighborhood that would have awed James Bond."

"I'll bet," Paula agreed crisply. Bernadette Carstairs spent half her life at her living room window, watching the comings and goings of people on the street. Now that this virtual stranger had talked to Bernadette, Paula told herself, he undoubtedly knew more about her private life than the Internal Revenue Service and the Federal Bureau of Investigation put together.

"My name is Ben, Ben Gallagher."

Looking down at the large hand he was holding out toward her, Paul shifted her package and extended her own slim one. "How do you do, Mr. Gallagher."

"I'm doing fine, but I won't really feel properly welcomed to Parcel Court until you drop the mister stuff and call me Ben."

As her cool fingers lay briefly in his, Ben studied the woman before him. He'd liked the look of her from the first. Perhaps she wasn't beautiful, but he'd long ago lost interest in merely beautiful females. This woman had something else—character, intelligence, humor?

He wasn't sure, but there was something about her. It was there in the way she kept her slender, willowy body. He guessed that she must be at least thirty, but she didn't look more than twenty-five. She took care of herself, and he respected that. He'd watched her run, and he liked the elegant precision of her movements. In fact, "elegant" was really the word that described her best—not just the way she moved, but the way she looked and held herself. From her smooth gold eyebrows, clear skin, slim nose and high, full breasts to her long, graceful legs, she was elegant.

And then there was that mass of gorgeous blond hair. Though she had it tied back, he had no trouble imagining that it must be pretty spectacular when it was unbound. It made such an intriguing statement above the gold and green flecked eyes now studying him just a trifle warily. When the gossipy old busybody who lived up the street had told him Paula Kirk was a widow, he'd been sorry for her loss but very glad to hear that she didn't belong to someone else. Ms Kirk definitely interested him, and he wanted to get to know her better.

She was looking a little doubtful about his exaggerated plea to call him by his first name. "Do you and your wife plan to stay here long, uh, Ben?" She withdrew her hand and tucked it in the pocket of her shorts.

"I'm not married." His smile widened, flashing even teeth that were a startling white against the bronze of his lean face. "And yes, I intend to stick around. Since Columbia is close to Washington and Baltimore, the location is ideal for me. Besides, I like the pathway systems and the wooded areas that run between the cul-de-sacs." He glanced over his shoulder at the house behind him. "My lease has an option to buy. So if I'm comfortable here, it might well be a permanent arrangement." He cocked his head. "How about you? Have you lived here long?"

"Five years."

"Then you must know and like the area."

"Yes," she allowed. "I work for the county. There's been a lot of development in the past ten years in the area, but much of it is still rural," she explained, warming to a subject that was dear to her. "And the parts of it that have been left natural are beautiful. If you like the outdoors, there are some wonderful places to hike and explore."

Ben shifted his weight, his blue gaze never leaving her face. He was readjusting his original assessment that Paula Kirk wasn't beautiful. Her features were innocent of makeup, but she had good bone structure. Add a little color to those pale lips and high cheekbones, and she'd look like a model. But even without artificial aids, when her countenance was animated, it projected a kind of inner glow that was really quite breathtaking.

"I do enjoy the outdoors," he heard himself saying. "In fact, I'm a nature lover in a lot of ways. Perhaps you'd be willing to have dinner with me some night this week so that I can learn more about this part of Maryland."

Paula took a step backward, totally surprised by the sudden invitation. In the year and a half since Tim's funeral, she'd had to refuse the advances of several importunate males. Each time she'd been astonished, and not just because in some ways she still hadn't adjusted to the idea that she was no longer married. Why would three of the young bachelors in her department ask an over-thirty type like herself for a date when they had twenty-two-year-old, mini-skirted secretaries at their beck and call? It didn't make sense. But those invitations had all come from men with whom she worked and who were perhaps misguidedly taking pity on her. This was the first time someone she really didn't know had asked her for a date, and she was thrown off balance.

"I'm sorry, Mr. Gallagher...Ben. That really wouldn't be possible," she said a shade more coldly than was necessary because of her confusion. "Maybe some other time."

He smiled easily. "My schedule isn't crowded. Just tell me a convenient day, and I'll circle it on my calendar."

Firmly Paula shook her head, and Ben's eyes narrowed as he saw the way the light was caught and trapped in her vibrant ponytail.

"I just can't do that right now," she insisted. "Sorry." She took another step backward. "Well, uh, have a good day, and I'll probably be seeing you around." Quickly she pivoted and walked away, her carriage very upright and the sheaf of hair tied at her back bouncing and shimmering in the strengthening morning light.

"See you," Ben repeated under his breath. He stood with his feet planted wide apart and watched her round the corner. What a wary creature she was, he thought, his gaze lingering on the firm, tanned thighs below the cuff of her white shorts. When she was out of sight, he shook his head. He was by nature and training an observant man. The moment he'd mentioned that he wasn't married, Paula Kirk's beautiful hazel eyes had become guarded, and when he'd invited her for dinner, she'd stiffened up. Why, he wondered. What was it about socializing with unattached members of the opposite sex that made her start to look like a rabbit that had suddenly come face-to-face with a hungry wolf? He didn't know, but there was no question about it—he was intrigued.

A few minutes later Paula pushed open her side door and stepped into the kitchen. Nat, wearing only pajama bottoms, was bending anxiously over the twenty-gallon tank on the bookcase next to the sliding glass door.

"Rapunzel looks sick," he pronounced without looking up. "There's a white thing on her side."

Paula rolled her eyes upward. Nat spent more time worrying about his favorite angelfish than a new mother with a colicky baby. "Maybe it's just a piece of fish food that got stuck to her."

"I don't think so."

Paula started unloading her grocery bag. "Even though I think they're too darn sugary, I bought your favorite cocoa flakes," she said brightly in hopes of distracting him.

The ploy worked, and a moment later Nat was perched on the stool in front of the counter, hungrily spooning up cereal. "Been running?" he asked around a mouthful of Captain Crispy.

"Yep. I jogged up to Martin Square." Paula eyed her ten-year-old son fondly. With his straight hair, freckles and long, slight build, he looked so much like her that they might have been brother and sister. Only his sweet smile occasionally reminded her of Tim. Every now and then when Nat looked at her in a certain way, memories of her husband pierced her like a knife. But, undeniably, the pain was less sharp now. With a determination and resilience that surprised even Paula herself, she was rebuilding her life. And she thought she was doing a pretty good job.

"I want to leave for work in half an hour," she told Nat. "Are you going to be ready for day camp?"

"Sure. It doesn't take me as long to get dressed as it does you."

Paula reached over and tousled his fair mop. "That's true, but all you do is step into your sneakers and pull on a pair of shorts. I have to make myself beautiful."

Over the top of his cereal spoon, Nat grinned back at her impudently, the freckles on his nose standing out like a brown sugar starburst. "Oh, yeah? Well I guess that explains why it takes you so long."

Refusing to comment, Paula headed for the staircase. Nat might enjoy teasing her, but the truth was that she'd learned to be very efficient about time.

Twenty minutes later, her hair coiled on top of her head and wearing a designer denim skirt and a deep blue cotton knit top, she watched as Nat scrambled into the passenger seat of their aging VW camper. Nat had nicknamed it the Blunderbus, and that was the way Paula thought of it now.

"Would you like to spend the weekend with Grandma?" she inquired of him as she backed out of the driveway. "She called to invite you last night."

"Sure. Whenever I come, she's got a freezer full of chocolate ice cream."

Shooting Nat an exasperated grin, Paula shifted from reverse and headed out of the court. As they rounded the corner, Ben Gallagher emerged from his garage and waved.

Nat waved back enthusiastically and then turned toward his mother. "Have you met the new guy who lives there?"

"I ran into him when I was coming back from the store," she admitted cautiously.

"He's really neat. He's the one who's bought the pet store up at Martin Square. He told me he'd show me his tropical fish when he finishes getting all his tanks set up." Nat's eyes suddenly lit. "Hey, maybe I can talk to him about that spot on Rapunzel's side."

Paula's eyebrows began to lift. Proprietor of a marginal pet shop was the last thing for which she would have pegged Ben Gallagher. "I don't want you bothering our new neighbor."

Nat was insulted. "I'm not bothering him. He's just a nice guy, that's all. And we have the same hobby."

The Blunderbus paused at a stop sign, and Paula slanted her son a brief glance. Nat had pretty good instincts about people and he was probably right. What harm was there in letting him talk to the man about fish? Just because Ben Gallagher had asked her for a date, that didn't make him the Boston Strangler.

After leaving Nat at day camp, Paula drove to the county building where she worked as director of the recreation program. Considering that she had been an English major until she dropped out of college at the age of nineteen to marry, it was an unlikely job. But it was one she enjoyed. She'd always been athletic and loved camping and backpacking. Through an interest in hiking the Appalachian Trail, she'd gotten to know some of the people in the recreation department and had been asked to lead a number of outdoor expeditions. Then, half a year ago, when the former director moved out of state, he'd recommended her for the position.

She would always be grateful for that piece of luck. The opportunity had come at a time when she'd desperately needed an anchor. And the job had proven to be exactly that. For the past six months she'd thrown herself into her work with an enthusiasm that was beginning to produce very gratifying results.

When she left the office late that afternoon, her mind was still so much on her work that the scorching temperature outside her air-conditioned building came as a shock. Getting inside the camper, which had been sitting in the parking lot, soaking up heat for the better part of the day, was like sliding into an inferno. The plastic steering wheel burned her palms, and she could actually see waves rising from the blacktop.

Two hours later, after she'd had dinner with her mother and dropped Nat for the weekend, she had to repeat the ordeal. When she finally maneuvered her unwieldy vehicle out onto the main road and headed toward home, she felt as if she were awash in her own perspiration.

All during the short drive, Paula's thoughts were fixed on the prospect of a refreshing shower. Yet, as she turned into Parcel Court, her gaze lingered for a moment on the rental house at the corner. Then even though she was eager to get out of the simmering heat, after she'd pulled the camper into the garage and hauled down the door, she paused to glance over at the spot where she'd seen Ben Gallagher early that morning. His house, like everyone else's, was shut up tight against the heat, and she wondered if he was at home.

In fact, several times during that day, her mind had drifted away from her work and she'd found herself thinking about him. Turning, she unlocked her front door and sighed with relief at the air-conditioned coolness inside. Then she went upstairs, shed her sticky clothes and directed her steps toward the bathroom. There she twisted on the taps in the shower. As she stood letting the water wash the heat and grime from her slim body, Ben Gallagher's image popped into her wayward thoughts yet again. This time she allowed herself to dwell on it for a moment or two.

He was definitely the most attractive man she'd met in a long time, she conceded. And unlike the under-thirty bachelors in her office who'd been pursuing her, he wasn't too young. Picking up an oval bar of scented soap, she began to slowly rub it over her body. As was her habit, she started with the sensitive skin of her knees and thighs and systematically worked up to the plane of her small, flat belly and then to her delicately molded rib cage above her narrow waist. As she smoothed the lather in small, circular strokes, she paused, her fingers grazing the curve of her breast. Since Tim's death, she really hadn't given much thought to whether the men she encountered were attractive or not. She hadn't been thinking in those terms.

Unconsciously her hand lingered on her breast for a moment or two while she considered that. Then, frowning slightly, she moved her hand from her breast and filled her palm with shampoo.

Since she'd lost Tim, she simply hadn't had any interest in dating and had politely but firmly repulsed all suggestions that she should. She was aware that when she'd turned down Ben Gallagher's dinner invitation, her refusal had been almost a programmed response. Several times during the day, however, she'd questioned it.

Now she did that again. She really was single, after all. Dinner with Ben Gallagher might be enjoyable. She had been a widow for more than a year now, and it had been a long time since she'd dressed in her best clothes and sat across the table from a good-looking male. But then Paula shook her head sharply. Men like Ben Gallagher didn't ask widows out because they enjoyed watching them eat. He would expect something more than casual companionship.

Paula thought that she just wasn't ready for that sort of entanglement with any man, much less a neighbor. Though she was still grieving for Tim, she was beginning to enjoy her new, relatively unencumbered lifestyle. She'd been married so young that she'd never really had a chance to find herself in the way that so many women were doing nowadays. Now that was beginning to happen, and she was so busy coping with the whole experience that she really hadn't the energy to make room in her life for anyone but Nat.

What's more, a widow with a young son had to be careful of her reputation, she told herself. Paula laughed aloud as another thought struck her. If she started fooling around with a sexy-looking bachelor who lived on Parcel Court, Bernadette Carstairs would have a field day. Anything was better than that, even continuing to live like a nun! And, anyway, she wouldn't know what to do on a date. No, for now at any rate, it was better to play it safe and keep men like Ben Gallagher at arm's length.

For several more soothing minutes, Paula stood beneath the spray, letting the warm water sluice the shampoo from her abundant tresses. Then she turned off the taps, stepped out of the shower stall and began to rub herself dry. When that was done, she slipped on a terry cover-up and then plugged in her hair dryer. Five minutes later she was standing dreamily before the bathroom mirror, trying to think how to reword a paragraph in a grant request for her pet project, the wilderness program. It was then that the lights went out and she was abruptly plunged into darkness.

"Oh, no," Paula groaned, unplugging the useless hair dryer and feeling her way out of the pitch-black bathroom. Last year, power failures during heat waves had been common. So far this summer there hadn't been any. Apparently, tonight her luck had run out.

And so had the luck of everybody else on the street, she realized after she'd felt her way downstairs and stepped outside. Parcel Court was eerily silent, and though it was dusk, there wasn't a lit porch light in sight. The air was still breathlessly hot. With all those air conditioners suddenly silenced, the inside of everyone's house would be hot pretty soon, too. Already some disgruntled householders were coming outside. Bernadette was one of the first to hit the street. Her eagle eyes spotted Paula right away.

"Did your electricity go off, too?" she shouted in a voice that never failed to grate.

When Paula admitted that it had, Bernadette began a high-pitched tirade against the electric company. "We should all sign a petition!" she railed. "Will you show your community spirit by coming over tomorrow to help me make one up?"

Paula crossed her fingers behind her back and excused herself. "I have to work tomorrow," she fibbed, and then slipped around the side of her house before Bernadette could say more.

Once safely hidden in her backyard, Paula inspected a bed of orange daylilies that were now blooming in profusion and pulled a few weeds in Nat's sadly neglected vegetable garden. Then she settled herself on the chaise longue that dominated the patio and began to run a comb through her damp hair. Actually, now that the sun was nearly down, it wasn't a bad time of day to be outside. The evening air was drenched with the perfume of late-blooming roses, and already fireflies were beginning to flicker in the shadows.

A short time later, Paula was still enjoying the evocative quiet when it was broken by the sound of footsteps. Over the top of her fence, she saw Ben Gallagher's head and muscular shoulders appear. He was wearing a crisp white short-sleeved shirt that enhanced the healthy darkness of his skin and that seemed to glow faintly in the waning light.

"Hello there."

"Hello," she answered, straightening.

"I'm looking for asylum. I couldn't stay in my house anymore. But when I came outside, Bernadette tried to inveigle me into heading a bomb squad and swearing vengeance on the electric company. Ferocious women terrify me, so I took the coward's way out and vamoosed." He grinned engagingly. "I see you were washing your hair when the plug was pulled."

"Yes," she admitted, and then put her comb down in her lap.

As Ben studied the picture she made, his pupils dilated in the thickening dusk. Propped very upright, with her long tresses flowing around her shoulders, she looked like a queen, he thought. Only the regal effect was spoiled somewhat by the short yellow terry shift she wore. It was probably knee-length when she stood, but now she was sitting, and it just barely covered her thighs, so he was presented with a very fetching view of her long, slim, but nicely curved legs.

Over the years, he'd found that in uncertain situations, it was often better to take the initiative. Since she wasn't issuing any invitations, he decided to trust his instincts. Smoothly undoing the latch on the gate, he strolled in. "I don't want to venture back into Bernadette's hostile territory just yet, and there's nothing else either of us can do until the electricity goes on, so do you mind if I join you?"

Paula was unable to think of a single excuse that wouldn't sound rude.

"Of course," she murmured and once more felt faint prickles of alarm running up her back as she watched him stride toward her.

2

As Ben Gallagher settled himself in the chair opposite Paula, she found herself once more taking a detailed mental inventory of his appearance. He had exchanged the brief corduroy shorts he'd had on early that morning for a pair of khaki Bermudas. They were several shades lighter than his hair-darkened calves and ankles. Against his white shirt, his tanned throat and face presented another contrast. And then there was the silvery blaze of his hair and the glint of ice-blue eyes below level black brows.

His feet were protected only by leather thongs, Paula noted before glancing down at her own toes. They were quite bare, as was the rest of her under the terry shift, she suddenly realized. Casting a slightly alarmed glance up into Ben Gallagher's aquiline features, she hoped he wouldn't guess.

"I'm afraid summer blackouts are a fairly common occurrence around here," she remarked.

"So I'm told." After crossing one bronze calf over his knee, he cradled his hands behind his head and regarded her. "How long do they usually last?"

"Not more than an hour."

"Hmmm." He smiled, his gaze drifting appreciatively over Paula. She had the dewy look of a woman who'd just stepped out of a shower. He could see from the drape of that shift over her full breasts that she wore no bra beneath it. What else was she not wearing? The sudden speculation produced a picture in his mind of Paula naked. Though he managed to control his almost instantaneous physical reaction to that, he couldn't quite control the caressing note in his voice when he murmured, "Summer blackouts could be more of an advantage than a nuisance if they afford me an opportunity to get to know some of my neighbors better."

"I was under the impression that you'd already met most of the people on the street."

"Meeting someone and getting to know them are two different things. I've met you, but I don't know you. I'd like to, though," he added, meeting her eyes steadily. "Very much."

Paula felt herself flush slightly. That was a quite direct assault. Ben Gallagher wasn't the shy type. She was thankful for the gathering twilight, which provided a measure of protection from that piercing blue gaze of his. There was a wicked glint in it that made her wonder what was going on in his mind. She looked away. "I hope the blackout hasn't seriously inconvenienced you."

He merely smiled. "If it just lasts an hour or so, it's not a problem. Longer than that, and it could be. I'm an aquarist and I've just finished setting up several breeding tanks. It's a delicate operation, and since my breeders have already been subjected to a lot of stress while I was moving in, I'd like to have the equipment functioning again as soon as possible."

She was interested in that. "My son is a budding aquarist." Paula smiled wryly. "He worries over his tank of fish like a mother hen. This morning he was moaning because he thought there was something growing on Rapunzel."

When Ben lifted an inquiring eyebrow, Paula explained with a little laugh, "As in, Rapunzel, Rapunzel, let down your long fins. She's one of his favorite angelfish."

"I see." Ben leaned forward. "Spots can be pretty serious, you know. If you like, when the lights go on I'll take a look."

Paula was startled by the offer. "That's very kind of you."

"Not at all. I met your son the other day," he went on. "Nice boy."

"Thank you."

"It can't be easy for a woman to raise a boy alone. But you seem to be doing a very good job."

Fireflies had come out in earnest and were winking in the darkness like tiny signal fires. Paula focused on one of them. "Thanks," she said again. "My husband was ill for a long time before he died. It was . . . it was very hard on Nat."

"Hard on the both of you, I'm sure," Ben commented. He didn't ask her any more about her husband's death. Bernadette Carstairs had already told him that Tim Kirk had spent two years wasting away from kidney failure, so he knew that Paula had been through a harrowing ordeal.

It was not a story that she wanted to be reminded of. Paula searched her mind for a way to change the subject. "Nat says that you're opening up the pet shop in Martin Square. I have to admit that I'm surprised."

"Why?"

"I don't know. Somehow you don't look like a man who would own a pet store."

Ben grinned at her. "What do I look like then?"

"You look like a man of action," she said, studying his athlete's body, the lines of experience in his face and the dry humor and keen intelligence behind those crystal-blue eyes. "You look like an adventurer, like a man who's been around."

"You're very observant and you're right," he returned evenly. "I have been a rolling stone. For the past decade or so I've spent a lot of time in equatorial climates. As a matter of fact, I first got interested in tropical fish by seeing some of them in their natural habitat in the Lower Amazon region."

Paula's eyebrows shot up. "Goodness, you have led an unusual life! What were you doing in the Amazon?"

"This and that." He steepled his fingers. "It doesn't matter. I've retired from that sort of thing and I intend to live very differently from now on."

Though she didn't ask any more questions, Paula's curiosity was piqued. In the Washington area, one was constantly running into people who worked for secret government agencies, who traveled a lot and who never discussed their occupations except in the most general terms.

She guessed that Ben Gallagher was some sort of secret agent who had decided to make a break with his past. It wasn't so unusual for men his age to wake up feeling dissatisfied one morning and to change their jobs and their life-styles. But she couldn't imagine that someone with his background wouldn't quickly find life in this quiet suburban neighborhood boring. Her guess was that the pet store and the house on the corner would probably be unoccupied again before long.

"Will the shop at Martin Square be the first you've owned?" she inquired politely.

"Yes. It's a kind of experiment for me, you see."

"I have to warn you that it hasn't exactly been a money-maker in the past. I think it's gone through three different owners in as many years."

"I'll take my chances." Actually, as far as he was concerned, the pet shop was something he was getting into just for the fun of it. He made enough money from consulting and from his investments that he didn't need to worry about profit margins.

"And if it doesn't work out?" Paula queried.

"Then I'll try something else."

There was no opportunity for more questions because just then the velvety quiet of the evening was shattered by the abrupt reawakening of dozens of air conditioners. Lights all over the street snapped on, and Paula turned her head sharply as a bright beam from her kitchen window suddenly penetrated the darkness.

Ben chuckled and then commented, "Well, it looks like I won't have to bomb the power company after all."

"No," Paula agreed. "Everything's back to normal. It really didn't last much more than a half hour, did it?"

"No, so it won't take our houses long to cool off again." He started to get out of his chair. "Thanks for the sanctuary from Bernadette and for the conversation. I'd better check to make sure my breeders are okay." He paused and looked down at her questioningly. "Which reminds me, I said I'd have a look at your son's fish. Would you like me to do that now?"

Paula hesitated. "Oh, it's not necessary," she started to say. But her voice faltered. Nat had really been worried about Rapunzel. "Well, if you've got the time to just take a quick peek, I would be grateful."

"Sure." He followed her as she opened the sliding glass door into the family room. Once inside, he knelt and peered into Nat's tank.

"There are some nice-looking specimens here, but I'm afraid your son's right," he finally said. "The angelfish is in trouble."

"What's wrong?"

Ben straightened. "It looks to me like an infection called microsporidia."

"It sounds dreadful. Is it serious?"

He nodded. "Unless it's treated right away, it attacks the organs and death results. It's also very contagious."

"You mean Nat's other fish might get it, too?" Unconsciously Paula wrapped her arms around her chest. Nat was crazy about the inhabitants of his aquarium. He'd gone through enough traumas lately without having his pets keel over on him. "Isn't there something I can do?"

"Yes. You can treat the tank with quinine sulfate. I have some at my place. You're welcome to walk over with me and get it if you'd like."

Paula looked from Ben's face back to Nat's tank. "I hate to impose on you."

"It's not an imposition," he assured her. "If you want to save your son's pets, you'd better medicate that aquarium right away."

That was all it took. "All right," Paula agreed. "Lead the way."

Five minutes later Ben Gallagher showed her into his house. As he closed the door behind them she looked around curiously. It was a three-bedroom ranch house with an L-shaped living-and-dining area. Since it was similar to a couple of other houses on the street, she was familiar with the floor plan. However, unlike those other, comfortably appointed homes, Ben's place was virtually unfurnished. Apparently the man hadn't acquired much baggage on his equatorial expeditions, she thought as she looked around at the bare wood floors and curtainless windows.

"Up until now I always traveled light," he commented, echoing her thoughts. "And when my wife left me a few years back, she took all the furniture with her."

Paula turned around. "You're divorced?"

"Yes. One time, when I'd been away on business for almost a month, I came back to find that my wife had walked out and found herself another guy. They're married and living in Denver now."

Paula's expression was sympathetic but also a bit startled. She'd guessed that he was divorced, but it was surprising to hear him blurt out such an ugly set of details so baldly.

Ben was surprised himself. He hadn't intended to tell her about Judy, but as he looked across the room at Paula standing there in her yellow shift like a willowy daffodil, he found himself wanting to tell her everything.

"That's tough," she said carefully. "It would be hard not to be bitter about something like that."

"I'm not." Ben's smile was dry. "I accept all the blame. Judy and I were married shortly after high school. We grew apart. The truth is, my job kept me away for such long stretches that I don't think any woman would have considered me much of a husband. If I'm bitter over anything, it's about Katy, my daughter."

"Oh?"

"She didn't see much of me when she was growing up, and when Judy took her away, we pretty much lost touch. Oh, there were letters and birthday presents, and occasionally I managed a visit, but..." His voice trailed off, and he went to the window and looked out, his broad shoulders drooping slightly. "It was my fault. My job demanded a lot, and I kept telling myself that she was just a baby and there was plenty of time." He shook his head. "But the time ran through my careless hands like water. Katy's eighteen, so it's too late."

When he fell silent, Paula took a step toward him. She wanted to offer him some comfort. "Even an eighteen-year-old needs a father," she said softly. "It's not too late for that."

"Yes," he replied, straightening slightly. "I've told myself as much. Now that I've settled down, I'd like to get to know her again. That's one of the reasons I rented this house instead of an apartment. Judy's agreed to let Katy come out East for college, and she'll be staying with me for a while before her semester starts. I wanted Katy to feel as if she were coming to a home and not just a bachelor apartment."

"Then you'd better buy some furniture," Paula suggested with a smile.

Ben turned toward her, a grin slashing his lean face. "Would you like to help me pick out a few pieces?"

"No, I think you should do that for yourself. But I'd be very glad to suggest some stores that sell nice things at reasonable prices."

He walked toward her, his shoulders once more firm and his stride confident. "I'd appreciate that." For a moment he stood smiling down at her. "You're a nice lady. Can I offer you a drink? There's beer in the refrigerator."

"I don't care for beer."

"Mine's homemade. Try it. If you don't like it, you can always spit it out in the sink."

She laughed at him. "No thanks."

A mischievous smile tugged at the corners of his mouth. "You're a nice lady but not very adventurous. All right, then come into the room where I keep my tanks. You can have a look at my breeders while I get that quinine sulfate for your son."

With a gallant flourish Ben took Paula's elbow and started to guide her toward the hall. It was the first time he'd touched her, and Paula experienced a small shock at the contact. During their talk, she'd almost forgotten the attraction that had made her so wary of him earlier. Then his suggestion that she help select his furniture had reminded her of it, and when his warm, dry fingers lightly grazed her skin, a tingling sexual awareness rushed over her. It had been a very long time since she'd experienced anything like that, and as he politely ushered her through a door on the right, she knew that her face was flushed.

Fortunately her host couldn't note her discomfort because the only light in the room they'd entered came from a series of aquariums mounted on wrought iron stands. In the semidarkness the blue-green underwater environments of the tanks shone with an otherworldly beauty. Their small, rainbow-hued inhabitants darted about inside like living flashes of brilliant color.

"Oh, how beautiful," Paula breathed, stepping away from Ben's grasp so that she could station herself in the middle of the room and look around.

"They are, aren't they?" he agreed in his deep voice. "So far, this is my favorite spot in the house. Stay here and enjoy. I'll be back in a jiffy."

He walked out, and when she knew he was gone Paula crossed her arms over her chest, feeling a curious mixture of relief and mounting apprehension. Just a little while ago she'd vowed to steer clear of Ben Gallagher. Yet here she was, alone with him in his house, an undeniable intimacy growing stronger between them with every passing minute. Where was this leading?

Annoyed with herself, she shook her head. She was a grown woman and he was a neighbor. Surely she could handle borrowing some medicine for Nat's fish from the man without feeling sexually threatened.

To distract herself from her thoughts, she began to walk around the room, admiring the beautiful aquariums. Each housed a pair from a different species, and though most were freshwater varieties, there were saltwater fish, too. Paula was no expert, but she recognized several fish of the type that Nat kept. There were neon tetras, tiger barbs, angelfish and bettas. She paused in front of each and then moved on. But when she came to a container that held a pair of discus fish, she lingered.

In the large, handsomely landscaped tank, the two creatures hovered near each other, their round, flat bodies trembling and their fins spread wide with what looked like barely suppressed excitement. Both were the same deep burnt orange, blending into brown on their backs, and both had eyes that gleamed in the translucent water like brilliant red rubies.

Fascinated, Paula moved closer and hunkered down to get a better look. There was no way to tell which of the two pancake-shaped creatures was male and which female. But one, Paula noted, had a greater girth. Did that indicate she was a female carrying eggs and ready to spawn?

With a sudden turn, the fish that Paula guessed was the male, swam around the slightly swollen female until he faced her. Then, to Paula's amazement, he pressed his mouth against the female's in what looked for all the world like an ardent and prolonged kiss.

Paula gasped and then rocked back on her heels when she heard the deep rumble of male laughter behind her.

"So Punch and Judy are at it again. I'm glad they've finally decided to get on with the show," Ben remarked.

"Is that what you call them? Punch and Judy?"

"Depends on my mood and theirs," he answered lightly, squatting down beside her where she now sat on the floor. "Sometimes they're Jack and Jill and sometimes Ma and Pa. Right now I'd say they were Romeo and Juliet."

Though the tiny hairs on the back of her neck seemed to lift in awareness when she felt the warmth of his large body so close to hers, Paula didn't look directly at him, but turned her face back to the tank.

"Are they actually kissing each other?"

"Not really, or at least not the way we think of it. Lip locking in fish is a kind of tug-of-war that plays a part in various phases of courtship behavior."

"Hmmm." Distracted by the activity in the aquarium, Paula made no further answer.

Abruptly the mouth-to-mouth contact between the fish ended. However, the male continued to hover close to the female, spreading his fins and trembling all over. At the same time the color patterns of his body changed and deepened so that the creature now had a brown-and-orange barred pattern that was clearly a glowing indication of his feverish sexual state.

"He's beautiful," Paula breathed.

"Yes," Ben agreed, his blue gaze on her profile rather than on the breeding tank. "They call a passionless person a 'cold fish.' But when courting, there's no more excitable creatures than certain types of fish. Salmon fight their way upstream against incredible obstacles. They die of exhaustion for just one brief moment of fulfillment. During mating rites, some species literally glow with passion. The love dance of the Siamese fighting fish really is poetry in motion."

Paula gave him a quick look. His face was very close to hers, and it occurred to her that it would be wise to get up and excuse herself now. But wisdom didn't seem to be her strong suit just at the moment. Lulled by his deep baritone, the low light and the fascinating scene before her, she stayed put.

"Right now Romeo looks like a living jewel," she said, pointing at the quivering male discus.

Ben turned back to the aquarium also. "Apparently his lady love thinks so, too. Look."

The couple had suddenly ceased their flirtation and were swimming around together, as though on a tour of inspection.

Paula cocked her head, and the small movement made her blond tresses, which had dried to a smooth curtain of pale gold, shimmer in the reflected light from the water. A long strand floated against Ben's arm and clung. Though the touch was lighter than gossamer, he was intensely aware of it and held his body still so as not to dislodge the fragile silken manacle.

"What are they doing?" she asked.

"The female has decided to accept her suitor, and now the couple are selecting a nesting site."

"Will they find one?"

"They ought to. I put that tile in for them."

"Oh, yes." Leaning forward, Paula moved her head again, and Ben almost sighed audibly as the satiny mass of her long hair drifted away from his arm.

"I see it," she exclaimed. "The one leaning against the back wall of the tank." She turned toward him and smiled in a way that made him ache. "How thoughtful of you."

"I'd better be thoughtful. I'm in the fish-raising business, remember?"

"Of course." Her smile widened, lighting up her eyes, which glowed with golden glints in the rippling aqua light. "What will happen to the lovers now?"

"They'll fix up their nest, lay eggs and watch over their brood—the same as all good parents."

Her expression grew thoughtful. "Love stories usually seem to end the same way, don't they?"

"In the books, maybe, but not always in reality. Nowadays, a lot of people don't find a 'happily ever after.'" He paused. "I didn't. And neither, apparently, have you."

Paula raised her hand in a small gesture of protest, her eyes huge in the pale oval of her face. "That's not really true. My marriage was happy until my husband died. I loved him very much."

"Then you must miss him very much."

"Yes."

Ben had told himself that he wouldn't touch her again tonight, that he would be the soul of discretion, but he couldn't seem to stop himself. Lightly, he laid a hand on her shoulder, feeling her soft skin next to his and the delicate bone structure beneath.

"Will you be angry if I admit that since talking to you this morning, I've been thinking about you a lot? I've been picturing you living in that big house with just your son, and I've been wondering if you're lonely."

She shook her head. "Why should I be angry? At least I've got Nat. I'm not alone. You live in a big house all by yourself."

"True," he agreed soberly. "And sometimes when I see the married couples all around me going two by two, I feel pretty isolated."

"In a way, everyone's isolated. It doesn't matter whether you're married or not."

"That's true, too," he said, thinking there was more to Paula Kirk than gorgeous blond hair and big, light-filled eyes. "But it helps to have someone you can talk to, share things with." No longer able to resist the temptation he'd been struggling against all evening, he stroked a hand down the silky length of her hair and then wove a fair strand through his fingers.

Paula shivered at the contact but didn't draw back. There was a heaviness in her body. Like a sleepwalker, she gazed up into his shadowy features, waiting with a sort of detached curiosity for what would happen next.

"It helps to have someone close to you, someone who'll be there when you need them," he said. His head moved closer so that their lips were only inches apart. "Paula, ever since I first saw you, I've been wanting to kiss you."

"You shouldn't."

"I know. But I can't always be wise. I'm lonely, too." His hand went to the back of her head, cradling it in his palm while his mouth found hers.

If he had grabbed at her or forced himself on her, Paula would have instantly fought free. But his light, almost friendly touch was infinitely more persuasive than coercion. She knew that if she pulled back, he wouldn't stop her. So, against her better judgment and in the strangely compliant mood his words had induced, she allowed herself to be cajoled.

It had been so long since Paula had been kissed by a man that the sensual pleasure of the experience surprised her. Ben Gallagher's firm lips felt good against hers—strong, warm and—yes—experienced. Undoubtedly he'd caressed many women this way. Though the kiss was gentle and exploratory rather than demanding, there was no mistaking the expertise with which he pursued his goal.

But she didn't care about that. During the long years since Tim's illness began, she'd simply forgotten this pleasure, and now she was too lost in the wonderful sensations Ben's kiss was producing to cavil. There were so many things to like. She was pleased by the slightly rough skin of his cheeks. Though he didn't press his body against hers, she could sense its wiry strength—

so different from her slender softness. Ben Gallagher was all male, and the female in her couldn't help responding to that.

She appreciated the smell of him, too—a heady mixture of mossy after-shave, soap and healthy male. And then there was the way his hand felt as it stroked her back and moved down to her waist and hip. How lovely to be touched by a man's hands, a man you liked, and to feel yourself warming like a flower kissed by the sun.

"I've just come to a conclusion," he whispered against her lips.

"What's that?"

"You haven't got anything on under this terry cloth dress."

Paula's hazel eyes opened reluctantly, and she looked into his blue ones with real regret. "No, I haven't. And I've just come to a conclusion myself."

"What?"

"That I must be crazy to be doing this."

"Then we're both a little crazy." He smiled. "But if power failures bring on this sort of lunacy, I could get to be very fond of them."

He started to lower his head again, but she turned her face away. "They don't usually," she said, struggling to her feet and starting to straighten her rumpled shift self-consciously. "In fact, kissing strangers isn't my usual sort of thing at all."

Ben stood up also. "I know that. You don't have to tell me." He laid a tentative hand on her shoulder. "But I think it's time you stopped thinking of me as a stranger."

She took a step backward. "What do you mean by that?"

"I only meant that I hope you'll reconsider my invitation to dinner. I don't think we were meant to be strangers. I want to get to know you better, Paula."

"No, I can't." She shook her head and turned to leave.

Surprised and puzzled by her refusal, Ben followed behind her. "What have you got against sharing a meal with me? I promise I'm offering perfectly wholesome food."

Paula continued on her way and didn't answer until she'd reached the door. "I know I wasn't acting like it a minute ago, but I'm not ready to start dating."

Ben stood looking down at her. He certainly agreed that back in the other room she'd seemed more than ready for a relationship. Aloud, he said, "I'd like to argue that point with you, but right now I suspect I'd be wasting my breath, wouldn't I?"

"Yes, you would."

He cocked his head. "If you change your mind, you know where you can find me."

"I know." She put her hand on the doorknob, but he reached out and covered her fingers with his.

"You're forgetting something."

"What's that?"

"The quinine sulfate." Gently, he pried her hand from the knob, unfolded the fingers and placed a small package in her palm. "Dissolve it in two hundred cc's of water. That should be enough to treat twenty gallons. Keep the solution in a dark place, and administer one third of the mixture on each of three days."

"Thank you," she said, looking down at where his hand still supported hers.

"You're welcome." He stepped to one side and opened the door. "And remember what I said. I'd like to get to know you, Paula. If you ever think you'd like to get to know me, you have a standing invitation."

3

"SO WHAT'S NEW with you these days?" Lynn Innes gave her daughter a searching, bright-eyed look.

Paula, who'd stopped by her mother's apartment to pick up Nat, replied casually. "Oh, nothing much. I've been working pretty hard on a grant to expand the wilderness program. You know that's always been my favorite."

Lynn made a face. "If there's nothing more exciting for you to tell me about, I'm sorry I asked. What did you do with yourself this weekend?"

Guessing where this might be leading, Paula studied her plump, pretty mother guardedly. "I led an overnight backpacking trip near the Youghiogheny River."

"Hmmm. Don't you think it's a little late in life for you to decide to turn into a tomboy?"

"This is the eighties, Mother. It's okay for women to do something besides needlepoint. What have you got against my job, anyway?"

"Nothing," Lynn sniffed. "It's just that you've become obsessed with it, and you don't leave time in your life for anything else."

Knowing only too well what that meant, Paula studied her mother with a jaundiced eye. Paula was tall and almost boyishly slim; Lynn, small and cuddly. Quintessentially feminine, Lynn loved nothing better than to spend her days baking and sewing and gossiping with her many friends. Her fine, straight hair had once been the same pale gold as Paula's, but it was now silver and cut in a pixieish style. That, together with her curvy build and bright eyes, made her look like an aging, but still very appealing, Tinkerbell.

"I met the most charming man down in the laundry room last week," she volunteered as she darted about straightening her already immaculate kitchen. "He's only thirty-five, just divorced and very lonely. The poor guy needs cheering up. If I invited him for dinner tomorrow night, would you join us?"

"No, I wouldn't. But you go ahead and invite him, anyway. When he tastes your cooking he'll fall in love with you, and younger men and older women are all the rage these days."

Lynn turned away from the sink and glared. Hiding a grin, Paula began to gather up Nat's things. Her silent laughter faded when her son suddenly looked up from the bowl of ice cream he'd been gobbling and said, "Maybe Gram could invite the new guy on the street. He's divorced."

Paula only had time to cast Nat a dark look.

"What new man?" Lynn was suddenly as alert as a squirrel sniffing a cat on the wind, and Paula braced herself. For the most part, she and her mother got along very well. Briefly, when Paula had still been frozen with grief over Tim's death, Lynn had talked about moving in with her. But both women had an independent streak and liked doing things their own way. It hadn't taken long for them to realize that living together wasn't the solution. There was now only one major source of friction between them. That was the not so subtle hints that Lynn had started dropping about Paula's dating again.

"Tell me about this new man," Lynn demanded. "Why have you been keeping him a secret?"

"There's no secret," Paula denied as she stuffed the last of Nat's comic books into a duffel bag. "He's just someone who's moved into that rental on the corner."

"He's going to run the pet store at Martin Square, and he likes tropical fish. He's real nice, too," Nat declared. Giving his stomach a satisfied pat and smearing chocolate ice cream on his T-shirt in the process, he pushed his empty bowl away. "While I was over here last weekend, he gave Mom medicine for Rapunzel, and it saved her life."

"Rapunzel's life, not mine," Paula clarified, eyeing the fresh stain Nat's sticky fingers had just produced. "I didn't have a white spot on my gills."

Lynn gave her grandson an indulgent smile. "Well, he does sound nice." Then she turned back to her daughter. "What do you think?"

"What should I think?" Paula was beginning to have that familiar beleaguered feeling. Once her mother started off on a particular track, she was about as easy to stop as a runaway locomotive under a full head of steam. "Yes, he seems very pleasant." Despite a valiant effort to appear unruffled, her hazel gaze slid away from Lynn's keen brown one. She was remembering Ben's kiss and thinking that "pleasant" was hardly the word.

"What's he look like?"

"Like a normal, healthy middle-aged man. He's tall with gray hair." The description hardly did justice to Ben Gallagher's appearance, but Paula wasn't going to tell her mother that the man across the street was somewhere around six feet—all of it lean muscle and wolfish good looks. Then she'd really be in trouble!

Lynn looked disappointed. "Gray-haired and middle-aged, hmmm. Well, even so, since he's being so nice to you and Nat, maybe I *should* invite him to dinner."

Now it was Paula's turn to glare. "You should do no such thing. Mother, this is not the answer to a maiden's prayer, this is just a man who lives across the street and is interested in fish. Please stop playing matchmaker."

"Well, someone has to do it," Lynn huffed. "You've been a widow for a year and a half, and in all that time you haven't made a single move to get out and see people."

"I see plenty of people," Paula gritted. Eager to make her escape, she grabbed Nat's hand and headed for the door.

"You know what I mean," Lynn persisted, following a pace behind and clearly having no intention of letting up. "You don't see the right kind of people."

"Mom, drop it. Why don't all three of us go out to a movie together next weekend, okay?" Leaning forward, she gave her mother a quick hug and then beat a hasty retreat.

"We sure left in a hurry," Nat complained as Paula pulled out of the parking lot. "I was going to ask for some more ice cream."

"You don't need any more. I'm surprised it's not oozing out of your ears."

Not appreciating the humor of this, Nat scowled. "Why don't you want Gram to invite Mr. Gallagher for dinner? I think that would be neat. Besides, he cured Rapunzel, so we owe him a favor."

Paula searched her mind for the right answer. In the week since she'd foolishly allowed Ben Gallagher to kiss her, she'd done her best to avoid the man, but Nat had been doing just the opposite. Delighted by the medicine Ben had sent, Nat had run across the street to thank him. Obligingly Ben had showed Nat his tanks. Since then, Nat had started calling Ben by his first name, and the two had become fast friends.

Now it seemed that every time Nat walked in the door, it was with a new bulletin about what Ben Gallagher was up to. One time he announced, "Guess what, Mom, he had to put the baby angelfish in a separate tank so their parents wouldn't eat them." Another time he told her, "Ben just bought a whole bunch of new furniture for his house, and it's really neat. He even got a water bed."

As she remembered that, Paula gripped the steering wheel and rolled her eyes. "A water bed, huh?" she muttered under her breath. "Well, that fits."

There wasn't much she could do about this unlikely friendship. Really, she was glad about it. Having a strong male role model would be good for Nat. She just wished that her idiotic behavior with the strong male in question hadn't made the situation awkward for herself.

Sighing, she turned to her son and said, "Tell you what, if you'd like to do something nice for Mr. Gallagher, why don't you offer to mow his lawn? I'm sure he's busy getting his store fixed up, so he'd probably really appreciate that."

Nat looked unconvinced. But Paula did her best to be persuasive, and finally he agreed.

"Okay, but I think he'd rather eat with us. He asked me once if you were a good cook."

Paula's eyebrows shot up. "Did he?"

"Yeah. He said he bet you were."

She pulled into the driveway and killed the engine. "And what did you answer?"

Nat grinned. "I said you used to be, but lately you just fix salads and hamburgers."

"I thought you liked the way we eat now."

"I do. I always hated those goopy casseroles and sauces you made. I'd rather have a peanut butter and jelly sandwich any old day."

"Well, that's a comfort." Paula slid out from behind the wheel while Nat scrambled out the other side. So Ben Gallagher wondered about her cooking. The information only strengthened her resolve to keep her distance. Nat was absolutely right. She no longer spent hours shopping, planning meals and hovering over a stove. Unlike her mother, she'd never really liked to cook. She'd just made herself do it because wives were supposed to. Now, with her job and her new life-style, those days were over. If Ben Gallagher was in the market for a lady friend to iron his shirts and fix him gourmet meals, he'd have to look elsewhere.

That night, as Paula brushed her hair, she eyed her image in the mirror and told herself that for a woman who was a mature adult, she was behaving like a fifteen-year-old. She was going to stop avoiding Ben and treat him just like any other neighbor. During the past few days, she'd built that kiss up in her mind until it was some sort of major passionfest, but really it was nothing—a mere aberration. The only sensible thing to do was just forget it.

True to her resolution, the next afternoon Paula walked out to the street's mail center without first checking to make sure that no one else was headed in the same direction. The person who cornered her in front of her mailbox, though, wasn't Ben Gallagher but Bernadette Carstairs.

"Where've you been hiding yourself?" the neighborhood gossip demanded.

"I've just been busy." Paula eyed Bernadette's bleached hair, which had been teased into such stiff and flawless symmetry that it almost looked as if she were wearing an upside-down lampshade. "It's so hot that everybody's been staying inside."

"I know," Bernadette lamented nasally. "Isn't it awful? But I heard on the TV that the weather is going to break in a couple of days, so we'll all get some relief. Which reminds me, didn't I see your son talking to the new man living at the Richardsons'?" she asked, referring to the elderly couple who owned the house Ben Gallagher had rented.

Feeling her face go stiff, Paula willed herself to relax. Bernadette's eagle eye was every bit as relentless as Lynn's. But Lynn meant well. Bernadette didn't, and her tongue could be dangerous. "Why yes," Paula answered carefully. "Nat's an aquarist, you know, and Mr. Gallagher is going to reopen the pet store at the shopping center."

Bernadette swooped down on that like a hungry condor. "Isn't that the craziest thing? A man like that? You've seen him for yourself, so you know what I'm talking about. I ask you, does he look the type to run a pet shop?"

Paula wasn't sure what her neighbor was getting at, but some instinct made her jump to Ben's defense. "I don't see what Mr. Gallagher's appearance has to do with it. Apparently the man likes animals."

"Oh, I just don't buy it." Conspiratorially Bernadette leaned forward. "Not only does he look like Clint Eastwood, but he has money, you know. The rent on that house isn't cheap, and the Richardsons told me he plunked down six months in advance, cash on the barrelhead. Just took it out of his wallet, unrolled a few big bills and dropped them on the table as if they didn't mean a thing to him, and there was plenty more where that came from."

Wondering how in the world Bernadette had learned this, Paula stared. The woman must have actually called up the Richardsons and pumped them for information, she realized.

"And he drives an expensive, brand new car," Bernadette was going on. "Do you have any idea what a BMW costs these days?"

When Paula shook her head, Bernadette rolled her eyes expressively. "Plenty! You know what I think?" she said. "I think that pet store is really a front."

"What?" Paula's jaw dropped.

"If I were you, I'd tell Nat to stay away from that man. I'll bet Gallagher is just using that shop as a front for something else, something slightly shady, if you know what I mean." Bernadette stepped closer so that suddenly Paula could smell her hair spray. "Who knows," the older woman speculated, "it could be anything—the Mafia, drugs. Maybe he's a spy or a detective who's been planted on the street to watch one of us. These days, anything goes."

"You're right," Paula agreed, grabbing her mail, locking her box and preparing to leave. "Nothing would surprise me anymore. Nothing at all!"

Three minutes later, when she was safely behind her closed kitchen door, Paula sagged against her refrigerator and started to giggle. Well one thing about Mr. Ben Gallagher, she told herself, he wasn't boring, and apparently she wasn't the only female on the street who was fascinated by him. In order to come up with her cockamamy spy theory, Bernadette must have been giving the man a lot of serious thought.

Paula put a hand up to her forehead. Maybe he *was* a spy. Hadn't he told her something like that himself? Perhaps he was building an atom bomb in his basement, or maybe he was breeding a new strain of tropical fish that would take over the aquariums of the world.

Grinning, Paula went to the phone book and checked a number. All week she'd been trying to work up the nerve to make an appointment for a haircut. Inexplicably her chat with Bernadette by the mailbox had put her in exactly the right mood to do it.

"I need a new look," she told herself after she'd set up a date for Friday morning. "It's time for a change in my life."

As it turned out, Bernadette had been right about one thing. Late Thursday night the searing heat wave that had gripped the area for almost two weeks finally broke. As was often the case, the abrupt change in the weather was heralded by a spectacular electrical storm that knocked down trees and power lines and left low-lying areas of the county temporarily flooded.

Friday, as Paula walked to Martin Square, she had to pick her way through puddles, tangles of fallen branches and wet leaves, but the pleasant temperature and fresh-smelling air was such an improvement that she didn't mind. When she arrived at the beauty shop, she found George, its diminutive Italian proprietor, rushing around in a panic. His power, which had been out most of the night, had only just come back on. As a result, he was behind on all his appointments.

"It'll be at least an hour before I can get to you," he explained regretfully. "We'll either set up another appointment, or if you want, you can wait."

Under ordinary circumstances Paula would have rescheduled, but she'd spent a lot of time talking herself into this haircut, and she was afraid that if she put it off, she'd lose her nerve. Furthermore, the morning was free. Nat had gone on a field trip with his day camp, and because of the extra time she'd put in over the past couple of weekends, she didn't need to go into the office until the afternoon.

"I'll wait," she told the apologetic little man. "But if you don't mind, I'll go outside. This is the first nice day we've had in what feels like forever, and I don't want to be indoors any more than I have to."

A section of the shopping center opened onto a small park with a fountain, and after she purchased a cup of coffee at the bakery, Paula headed for it. When she'd found an unoccupied bench and taken a sip from her cup, she looked around appreciatively. It was so lovely to see a sky that was clean and blue rather than hazy with smog and to be able to take a deep breath without having the feeling that her insides were being fried. The grass had been dried out by the heat, but last night's downpour had refreshed it, and already Paula could pick out hints of green.

She glanced around the enclosure. The pet shop was one of the stores lining the walkway. It wasn't open yet, but it looked as if work on it was going forward rapidly. Was there any chance she might catch a glimpse of the mysterious Mr. Gallagher? Though it had been days since she'd made any attempt to avoid him, she hadn't seen the man, and she'd even begun to wonder if he was avoiding her.

Glancing down into the depths of her cooling coffee, Paula tried to assess her feelings. She should be glad he was making himself scarce, she told herself. They were neighbors. If she'd had to reject another advance from him, it would have been embarrassing for both of them. So how come she was feeling irritated, she asked herself. And how come she was sitting here directly in front of the pet shop, where the man couldn't miss her if he should happen to look out the window?

But, as Paula discovered a few minutes later, Ben wasn't inside. He'd had to pick up a few items in the hardware store, so he didn't spot her until he came striding around the corner, toting a bag of light bulbs and six-penny nails.

Even though she was sitting with her back to him, he recognized her right away. Taking a deep breath, Ben veered from his path and started to cross toward her bench. He'd been on the run constantly for the past couple of weeks. Even so, he'd spent a lot of time thinking about Paula Kirk. Had she been returning the favor, he wondered. Maybe this would be a good opportunity to do a little detective work.

"Beautiful day, isn't it?"

Paula jerked her head around, almost spilling her coffee. Ben Gallagher, a quizzical expression on his deeply tanned face, was standing directly behind her. The sun, now fairly high overhead in the clear sky, highlighted every detail of his appearance and Paula stared. She'd forgotten how good-looking he was. In worn jeans that clung to his long legs and rode low on his hips, he was startlingly attractive. Above his jeans he had on a blue knit shirt that emphasized the color of his eyes and underlined the silvery glint of his thick, rather unruly hair.

"Yes, it is," she murmured.

"Are you just sitting there enjoying the weather or are you expecting someone?"

Paula lifted her cup in a mock salute. "I'm having some coffee while I wait for a hair appointment."

"Good idea. In fact, it's been a while since breakfast and I'd like a hot drink. I think I'll get rid of this bag and pick up some coffee." He gave her a quizzical look. "If I join you here to drink it, will you run away?"

Paula shook her head. "Of course not." What else could she have said, she asked herself as she watched him stride off. It was a free country, and she didn't own this bench. It would be rude to get up and walk away.

A few minutes later he was back, carrying not only coffee, but a couple of cheese Danish in a white bakery bag.

"Can I tempt you?" He took out one of the goodies wrapped in waxed paper and held it toward her.

The warm bakery fragrance reached out to Paula like a seductive perfume. "I've already had cereal and I don't need the calories," she demurred, but her eyes remained fixed on the offering.

Ben's gaze swept over her slim figure. "I don't think you need to worry about your weight. C'mon, just this once be wicked with me."

Paula's gaze darted from his hand to his eyes. They sparkled at her roguishly. Ben Gallagher's laughing eyes were irresistible, and suddenly she found herself chuckling at the obvious double meaning of his invitation.

"I'll be wicked with you so long as it's just calories we're talking about," she allowed, accepting the pastry and taking a bite. It was delicious and so was the cooling coffee she washed it down with and the day with its rain-cleaned air and bright colors. What was it about this man, she wondered. Before he'd appeared, the scene had been pretty. Now it was luminous, and her senses were registering it as if they'd just been plugged into a power booster. They were registering him, too, but she tried to ignore the fact. It wasn't easy with his knee only inches from hers and his arm resting casually along the top of the bench behind her.

"I've been wanting to thank you for being so nice to Nat," she said. "I hope he hasn't been making a nuisance of himself."

"He's a nice kid. I've enjoyed having someone to talk fish with."

Paula slanted him a look, wondering if he were joking. But his blue eyes were now guileless, so she let the remark pass. Ben had already made short work of his own treat and was leaning back to enjoy his coffee. "You said you were waiting for a hair appointment."

"Yes," she volunteered. She swallowed the last morsel of Danish and started to lick a crumb from her finger. "I've decided to get my hair cut short."

Ben had been focusing on the crumb of frosting decorating the tip of her tongue, but the moment she mentioned the word "cut," his gaze jerked back to her face.

"You're kidding!"

Surprised by his vehemence, Paula shook her head. "No, I'm over thirty now, and I think it's time."

"Time for what?"

"Time for a more mature look. Only kids wear their hair long like this. I should have had it chopped off years ago."

"Why didn't you?"

Beginning to be a bit put off by the rapid-fire inquisition, Paula set down her empty coffee cup. "Well, I considered it a couple of times, but..." Her voice trailed off, and she stared at him curiously.

"But your husband wouldn't let you do it, I bet."

"How did you know?"

"That's simple. I knew because, if I were your husband, I wouldn't let you do it, either." His bright blue eyes shifted to her throat where several pale strands had become tangled inside her collar. Plucking at one of them, he caught it gently between his long, brown fingers. "Lady, how can you even think of cutting off gorgeous stuff like this?" he asked gruffly. "It would be a crime against nature to violate it with scissors. I won't let you do it."

Laughing a bit uneasily, Paula pulled the hair from his grasp. "Well, I'm afraid there's not much you can do." She glanced at her watch. "In another fifteen or twenty minutes George ought to be ready to take me."

I'm ready to take you right now, he thought. Aloud, he said, "Since you have a few minutes, how about having a look at the work I've done in the shop?"

When Paula hesitated he leaned forward and growled teasingly, "C'mon. I'm about to select paint colors; I could use some advice from a woman with good taste."

"How do you know I have good taste?" Paula asked as she got up from the bench.

"I don't. And frankly, since you told me what you're planning to do with your hair, I'm beginning to have misgivings. But I like your looks, so I'm willing to give you the benefit of the doubt." He took her arm and began to lead her toward his boarded-up pet store. "Come into my parlor."

"Said the spider to the fly?"

Paula pulled back slightly and Ben's white teeth flashed. "Said the lonely bachelor to the gorgeous blonde. Or have I just made it worse?"

She felt herself getting slightly warm, but at the same time she couldn't help being intrigued and amused. "Definitely."

"All right then, let me revise that to 'said the nervous new store owner to a prospective customer.' Better?"

"It would be if I believed you," Paula retorted smartly.

He pushed open the door, and she realized that she was grinning from ear to ear. *I'm flirting,* she thought with a little jolt of surprise. *And I'm enjoying every minute of it.* How long had it been since she'd felt light-hearted enough to flirt? She couldn't remember and hadn't even thought she was still capable of it.

"What do you think?" Ben asked, switching on a fluorescent light and then making a sweeping gesture.

He really had done a lot of work. The place smelled of plaster and fresh sawdust. The shelving was new and so was the quarry tile floor.

"I suppose it's because you've still got the windows boarded up, or maybe it's because it faces north," Paula said after she'd complimented him on his renovations, "but it seems kind of dark. Do you plan to use bright colors in here to counteract that?"

"Nope." Ben moved toward the center of the room and watched while Paula walked around the perimeter, examining his carpentry. "My store is going to cater primarily to the tropical-fish trade, and too much light will promote algae in the tanks. In fact, I thought I'd paint the walls dark blue or aqua."

Over her shoulder, Paula glanced back at him. Obviously he'd already decided on a color scheme and didn't really want her advice.

"Do you think you can make a living from aquarium supplies alone?" she asked. "The last couple of owners who went out of business here sold all kinds of animals—puppies, kittens, gerbils, guinea pigs. There was even a python over in that corner," she added with a little shiver. Actually, because of the sinister-looking creature, she'd always avoided coming into the store.

Ben took several steps toward her, a small smile quirking the corners of his mouth. "Pythons like their food live. You feed one by keeping a mouse in its cage. Softhearted types like me don't care to sit around watching doomed mice. Actually I don't approve of keeping puppies and kittens in cages in order to sell them, either. I think I'll stick to fish."

"But how . . ." Paula started to ask, then let the sentence die. What was it to her whether or not he went bankrupt? According to Bernadette, the shop was only a front, anyway. Maybe the woman was right. Maybe Ben Gallagher was really a bookie or in the numbers racket. He looked tough and savvy enough for either. And right now, with those wicked blue eyes sending shivers down her backbone, he looked threatening in another way.

He'd taken several more leisurely steps toward the corner where she was standing. "You don't seem to think much of my business sense. Are you afraid I'm going to starve?" He wondered if he should tell her that the pet shop was only a hobby. But then she might ask what he *really* did for a living, and the consulting work he was now doing for his old department was extremely sensitive and top secret.

"No," Paula replied. She swallowed as he moved even closer. "You look to me like a man who can take care of himself."

"I am," Ben agreed. "I'm also a man who knows what he's doing." He was now less than a foot away. Leaning forward, he flattened his hands against the wall on either side of her. "What am I doing?"

Paula looked at one of the muscular arms that were now imprisoning her shoulders.

"It's been a while for me, but I'd say you were making a pass."

Slowly he shook his leonine head and a thick, silvery lock fell forward. "Not yet. That might come later. Right now, I'm getting ready to plead my case."

"What case?"

The corners of his mouth twitched, but his blue eyes were solemn. "I don't want you to cut your hair."

Paula blinked, thrown off balance by his sudden change of mood. "Why not?"

"Because it will break my heart."

She didn't know whether to laugh or take him seriously. Finally she compromised by saying as lightly as she could, "That's a little hard to believe, when we hardly know each other."

His level gaze didn't waver. "True, but I'm working on it. I've already fallen in love with that long yellow hair of yours. If you cut it off, you'll spoil a lot of very fine fantasies."

"Oh, come on!"

"I never lie. What did you do last night while thunder was crashing around all our houses and rain poured down like it was the end of the world?"

"Slept through it."

"Not me. Storms are my thing. I opened my window, lit a cigarette, poured myself a brandy and stared out at nature's fireworks for what seemed like half the night. And when threads of lightning split the sky, know what I thought of?"

Mutely Paula shook her head.

One of his hands moved away from the wall and went to the back of her neck. "How this would look spread against black velvet."

Ben knew that what he'd just told her must sound a bit ridiculous. The trouble was that it was actually true. Smiling half at himself and half at the situation, he very gently unsnapped her barrette and twined her long tresses around his wrist.

Paula told herself to object, but she couldn't move an inch. There had been something so intimate in the gesture that she felt herself tremble inwardly. Struggling to recover from its effect on her, she stood statuelike. Ben had begun to spread her hair around her shoulders, arranging it as if he were an artist who meant to paint her portrait.

"It will give me nightmares if you cut this lovely stuff," he said quietly. "Don't do it."

"You've got a line from here to the moon. I don't believe a word you're saying," Paula managed. But even to her own ears, her whisper sounded tremulous.

"I never lie," he murmured, "and the moon is exactly where I'd like to be right now. How about you? Care for a little space walk?" Putting his hands around her waist, he began to draw her toward him.

Paula had known for quite a while that Ben Gallagher intended to kiss her again. She'd suspected it even before he ushered her into the store, and when they were inside and he'd started walking toward her like a wolf closing in on an unwary doe, she'd been absolutely certain. She was also well aware that up until this moment, she'd had plenty of opportunity to escape. Even now, if she really wanted to, she could easily break away.

Somehow, though, that didn't seem like the thing to do. And when his mouth took hers, escape seemed downright absurd. She'd been fibbing when she'd claimed to have slept through that storm the previous night. Oh, she'd been asleep through part of it, but for a good long time she'd lain awake in her lonely bed, listening to the cracks of thunder echo like enemy artillery fire and wondering what it would be like to have Ben Gallagher's arms around her.

Now she knew. It felt very good indeed, better even than she'd remembered—and that hadn't been half-bad. His kiss was as good as she remembered, too. His lips on hers were firm, aggressively masculine, yet at

the same time oddly friendly—not old-pal friendly—
but very exciting. Because, though there was a sense of
recognition, of rightness about his kiss, there was also
a lot of discovery going on and a great deal that was
very new.

Somewhere in the back of her mind, she couldn't help
comparing Ben with her husband. Tim had been a
good-looking man who, until his long illness, had
prided himself on keeping in shape. Ben, though no
taller, was leaner, harder. He felt different in other
ways, too. When he'd pulled Paula to him, she'd laid her
hands lightly on his upper arms. There, her fingertips
sensed a wiry, tense quality that was new to her. There
was something feral about it, as if he never truly relaxed, as if he were always prepared to spring.

Yet, as she began to succumb to his kisses and raised
exploring hands to the back of his neck, she found that
his hair was softer than she'd imagined. Despite its
springy thickness and metallic color, it was silky.

"This feels good," he whispered against her mouth.

"Yes," she agreed.

"Game for another round?"

"No."

"Yes, you are." To prove his point, he pulled her even
closer and lowered his head. This time his kiss had more
authority, and when he deepened it, Paula discovered
that he'd been quite right. She wasn't ready to back off
yet. His tongue teased her lips and then slid between
them. For a moment she resisted, but then opposition
began to seem pointless and she yielded.

When her teeth parted he made a little sound of satisfaction deep in his throat, and she felt his hands move
from her waist to the small of her back. One palm

stayed there, warm and supportive, but the other came up to her head, where he threaded his fingers through her loosened tresses.

She liked the feel of that. It was as if he held her prisoner, and yet at the same time her hair bound him as well. In their mutual pleasure and mounting excitement, they were both captives.

And there was no denying that the excitement was building—dangerously so. Blood was beginning to sing in her ears, and her skin felt warm and tingly. So lost was she in this welter of pleasant sensations that it was a moment or two before she noticed that Ben had moved his hand from her back in order to lightly stroke her breasts. He knew exactly how to touch a woman, and beneath the soft material of her jersey top, her nipples grew taut. But even though it felt very nice, Paula's warning system clicked on and she started to draw back.

Ben resisted. "Chicken."

"I think it's time we stopped this nonsense."

"It makes very good sense to me. It's quitting just when things are getting interesting that's illogical."

"Ben!"

"I'm not going to let you go until you promise me something."

She gazed up at him, aware how she must look— flushed face, her mouth swollen, her top in disarray. "What?"

"Promise me you won't cut your hair."

"Honestly, Ben!"

"I won't stop kissing you until you do. It's my fantasies you're threatening, you know. Any man worth his salt will fight like a territorial grizzly to protect those."

Instead of a bear, he looked like the devil's right-hand man, with those wicked blue eyes and that smile that could charm a toad. Once more all her defenses dissolved, and she started to laugh. "All right, you win."

"You won't cut it?"

"No, not today. I'll walk over and cancel my appointment right now."

"I knew you'd see the light."

"It's just self-protection. Anything is better than being ravished in a pet store, even having to brush this stupid mane of mine every night."

The tiny lines at the corners of his eyes crinkled. "Invite me over tonight and I'll brush it for you."

"Not on your life."

She turned away but he caught her hand. "Paula, there's just one more thing."

"What's that?"

"Have dinner with me this weekend."

She stared at him, not sure how she was going to answer. There was no very good reason why she shouldn't accept his invitation. Everything that was female in her wanted to say yes. Yet, at the thought of becoming involved with a man like Ben, another part of her quailed, as if she were made of straw and contemplating walking through a forest fire.

That was the part that prevailed. She shook her head firmly. "No. I know what you're thinking, but despite my little performance just now, I'm still not ready for what you're offering."

He released her wrist and put his hands on his hips. "How do you know what I'm offering unless you give it a chance? If you won't go out with me tomorrow night, at least take a rain check and promise me you'll think about collecting on it."

Paula hesitated. "All right," she finally said, "I'll think about it."

4

DURING THE NEXT FEW DAYS Paula only saw Ben a couple of times and only from a distance. The feeling of disappointment this engendered annoyed her. Surely if there'd been anything behind that elaborate line he'd spun out for her, she told herself as she cleared away the dinner dishes Friday night, he'd be making some attempt to persuade her to collect her "rain check." He knew the route to her backyard.

Damn the man, Paula thought, setting a pot in the sink and standing with her arms akimbo as she stared out the window. *He's doing nothing whatsoever for my peace of mind.*

She consulted her watch. It was time for Nat to come in. The two of them had a big day planned. Starting at eight the next morning, she was leading a "river splash" for the recreation department, and her son was coming along. Five minutes later he straggled in and switched on the TV.

"Where've you been?" Paula asked.

"At Johnny's. He's got a new dirt bike." Nat's eyes remained fixed on the violent cops-and-robbers show he liked to watch and of which Paula disapproved.

Well, at least he hadn't been over at Ben Gallagher's, she thought as she stepped forward to turn down the volume. "Listen, I want you in bed pretty soon. We have to get up at six-thirty tomorrow."

"Yeah, I know." Nat's gold-and-green-flecked gaze swiveled to hers. "Ben asked if we'd like to ride with him, but I told him he could come in the camper with us."

"What?" Paula was dumbfounded. Though she had the registration list for the river splash, she hadn't yet looked at the names on it. "Is he signed up?"

"Didn't I tell you he was?"

"No, you did not."

"Yeah, I told him he should because it would be really neat. He's taking Katy, too. That's his daughter. She's staying with him until she starts college."

"I see."

Quite unaware that he'd dropped a small bombshell, Nat turned back to his TV program. Paula stared at his tousled blond hair and opened her mouth. Nat had no business issuing invitations behind her back. But then she took a deep breath and stifled the reprimand. Why shouldn't she give Ben and his daughter a ride? Actually she was curious to meet the girl.

Not long after she'd tucked Nat away, Paula went to bed, too. She needed a solid night's rest, she told herself. Yet despite her good resolutions, she lay awake a long time, fretting about spending the day in Ben's company tomorrow. Just when her life had settled down, he'd come along and thrown it into disarray. She wasn't even sure why he upset her as much as he did. The man was attractive, so why didn't she just relax and see where that attraction led? But she knew where it would lead. That was part of what had her scared.

Turning over, she wrestled with her pillow, trying to pound it into a more comfortable shape. She wasn't ready for an intimate relationship with a man, she told herself. She wasn't the type for casual sex, and she was afraid of an involvement that went beyond the superficial.

Just then there was a tap on the door. "Mom?"

"Yes?"

"Are you awake?"

Paula sat up. "Yes. What's wrong?"

The door swung inward and Nat stood on the threshold. "I had a bad dream, and now I don't feel like going back to sleep."

Instantly alert, Paula patted the side of the bed. "Would you like to sit down and tell me about it?"

"Uh-uh." In the darkness she could just barely make out that he was shaking his head.

Paula didn't press him. She knew what his bad dream had probably been about. Nat had suffered through the agony of his father's illness, too. Watching Tim slowly deteriorate while they waited and hoped for a kidney transplant that didn't become available in time to save him had scarred her in ways she didn't even understand herself. Unfortunately it had had the same effect on Nat.

She got up and reached for her bathrobe. "Would you like me to read to you, honey?" She dropped a comforting arm around his shoulder and gave him a light squeeze.

He was stiff for a moment. Then he seemed to relax. "Could I have a cup of cocoa or something?"

"Sure," his mother agreed. "In fact, I'd like that myself. I'll fix us both a cup."

"Were you dreaming about Daddy?" she asked a little later as she and Nat perched on the stools in front of the breakfast bar.

"Yeah," he admitted, his gaze avoiding hers. "It was a really dumb dream, but when I woke up I felt bad."

"How do you feel now?"

"Okay. Sleepy, I guess. Maybe I'll stop watching that TV show you don't like."

Paula suppressed a grin. "Sounds like a good idea."

Nat looked sheepish. "I think I'll go back to bed now." He drained his cup, then looked up and gave her a smile. "Thanks, Mom."

At the risk of offending his ten-year-old dignity, she reached over and gave him a hug. "Anytime."

Together they climbed the stairs, and Paula insisted on once more tucking him under the covers. When she'd kissed her son on the forehead and switched off his bedside lamp, he said into the darkness, "I haven't had one of those stupid nightmares in a long time. I thought they were all done with."

"They're going away, Nat," she answered softly. "Maybe you won't have any more after this."

"I sure hope not."

She knew what he meant. After Tim had died she'd had a few nightmares herself. During his last days he'd been almost totally dependent on her. He'd hated it, and she'd hated knowing how he felt and not being able to change things. As she'd watched him slip away, she had been overwhelmed by irrational feelings of guilt. They didn't make sense, of course, but she couldn't help feeling that somehow, by being more perfect—a better cook, a better housekeeper, a better wife—she should have been able to stop the progress of his illness.

Her shoulders slumping, Paula padded to her room and slipped back into bed. Maybe she was beginning to get her life back on an even keel, but she knew that in a lot of ways she and Nat were still walking wounded. For both their sakes, it was simpler and easier to keep things uncomplicated. That meant this was not the time to consider becoming emotionally entangled with another man. It was better and safer all around to continue sleeping in an empty bed.

Her hand crept out to the untouched pillow at her side where Tim's dark head had once rested. Tears stung her eyes as she remembered the warmth and laughter that had filled their marriage before his illness. She was honest enough to admit, however, that there had sometimes been problems in their relationship. Tim had insisted she remain a full-time mother and housewife. Though she'd occasionally felt constrained by that, there had always been a great deal of love between them. Sometimes she missed him so much that it hurt. In a way it was shocking to find herself now sexually attracted to another man. What would she have thought of Ben Gallagher if Tim were still alive, she wondered. The question was disturbing because she really didn't know the answer.

Paula did finally get to sleep, but her rest was uneasy. When she stumbled out of bed at the crack of dawn, the image that greeted her in the mirror was so haggard that she wondered if she was up to the long day she'd scheduled. However, when Nat joined her for breakfast, his bright and smiling face showed no effects of his restless night.

At seven-thirty sharp the two of them came out of the house dressed in shorts and carrying a couple of bags

of supplies. They were just in time to meet Ben Gallagher, strolling up the driveway with a short, cuddly
redhead whose brilliant curls seemed to explode around
her head in a fiery aureole. The only similarity between Katy and her father was her blue eyes. As Paula
looked into her pretty, appealingly freckled face and
shook her small, warm hand, she felt a peculiar pang.
This girl takes after her mother, she thought. *This must
be how Judy looks.*

"I'm so glad to meet you, Mrs. Kirk," Katy said.
"Dad's told me all about you."

Paula shot Ben a curious look. What had he told his
daughter? And what was there to tell? But he only
smiled back at her serenely, his bland expression giving nothing away. Turning back to Katy, she said, "Call
me Paula, please. And I'm very glad to meet you, too."

After Katy and Ben slid into the back seat and Nat
ensconced himself in front, Paula drove to the spot
where she was to meet the others who'd signed up for
the expedition. Though Ben was mostly silent, she was
very conscious of him sitting behind her. It was Katy,
however, who kept the conversation going. The girl
was a bundle of questions. "How often do you lead day
trips like this, and what other kinds of field trips do you
go on?"

Paula rolled down the camper's window so they'd
have more air. It was still fairly cool, but the day
promised to be another scorcher. Since the heat wave
had broken a week earlier, the weather had settled
down to its usual late-July pattern—blazing sun, high
humidity and temperatures in the upper eighties and
low nineties.

"I go on a trip just about every other weekend, and the expeditions vary. In summer, for instance, there's rock climbing, spelunking, trail hikes, canoe and rafting trips, and even a couple of wilderness weekends. Next season I plan on scheduling a five-day bike trip."

"Oh, neat!" Katy exclaimed. "I like doing outdoor stuff. Back home I ski a lot and belong to a mountain-climbing club."

As she stopped for a light Paula glanced over her shoulder and smiled. It wasn't hard to picture Katy flying down a slope on skis, her brilliant hair flashing like a beacon. Without her intending it, Paula's gaze slid to Ben. Had he ever seen his daughter ski, she wondered. He'd admitted to missing most of Katy's childhood. Was he feeling a pang of regret now? And suddenly, as his eyes met hers, she knew that he was.

A half hour later Paula had picked up all the members of her small party and they were scrambling down an overgrown path at the side of a railroad bridge to a small sandy area just below. They chatted pleasantly, exchanging names and other bits of casual information, and Paula began to feel buoyant. Though the weather promised to be hot, it was going to be a beautiful day. The sun had burned off the last of the morning mist, and the sky was sapphire. Other colors stood out—the slightly paler blue of the cornflowers that bloomed amid thickets of yellow-green grass, and the deeper shades of the trees and bushes lining the verdant edge of the riverbank. By this part of the summer, Maryland lawns and flower gardens began to look faded, but here in the woods, with running water providing moisture, a lush, steamy freshness still clung to everything.

"Just exactly what are we going to be doing on this 'river splash'?" a middle-aged schoolteacher named Sarah inquired.

"You'll see," Paula said with a laugh. "It has to be experienced to be appreciated."

At her direction, everyone began to squat on logs and rocks to don the long socks and old tennis shoes that were part of the outfit she'd prescribed in the trip description.

Nat was the only one to grumble. "I don't see why I can't go barefoot."

"You will when we're in the water," Paula explained patiently. "Riverbeds aren't like a flat sand beach. They can have sharp rocks in them."

When she finished speaking she glanced to her right and found Ben's gaze on her. All morning she'd been trying to treat him casually, but when she realized that he'd been studying her body, she felt a slow flush begin to creep into her cheeks. He didn't look away when she caught him at it, either. Instead, his crystal gaze moved up to hers, and he smiled like a pirate contemplating an unbreached treasure chest. She found herself grinning back.

Ben was thinking that he was seeing a new side of Paula Kirk. He'd been slightly worried about the shadows under her eyes when he'd first seen her this morning. But they'd disappeared, and now, in a faded pair of navy cotton shorts and with her hair swinging against her back in a long burnished braid, she looked girlish. Her tennis shoes and her white knee socks that molded her well-muscled calves and contrasted with the golden tan of her firm, smooth thighs underlined the effect.

Then there was that red tank top. It was perfectly appropriate for the weather, and he knew she wasn't wearing it to be provocative. In fact, Katy had on something very similar. But on Paula, the thing was riveting. As he took in the thrust of her full breasts, he remembered how they'd felt crushed against his chest in the pet shop and how they'd seemed to swell when he'd stroked their lush contours.

It was obvious that the attraction was mutual. So why did she freeze up every time he tried to ask her out? He knew damn well she wasn't frigid or afraid of men. Surely, enough time had gone by since her husband's death that she wouldn't feel guilty about opening herself up to another male. Yet there was something, something that made her draw back from the flame springing up between them like a kid with burnt fingers. He wasn't into forcing himself on unwilling women. Because of that and the ferociously busy pace of his complicated life of late, he'd decided to give it a rest. If she wanted him, she knew where to find him.

So why, then, had he signed Katy and himself up for this trip? He knew perfectly well why. And so did Paula. It was because he wanted her and knew in his gut that, despite her senseless refusals, she wanted him, too.

When everyone was safely shod, she said, "Well, folks, the time has come. Follow me."

She had chosen a spot where at this time of year the river, though broad, was no more than a trickle. As she walked into it over the damp, rock-strewn sand, the water just barely covered the tops of her sneakers. Nat ran ahead of her, splashing enthusiastically. The others followed at a more sedate pace.

As usual, the adults were a mixed bag. In addition to Sarah, the schoolteacher, there were two sisters in their twenties named Liz and Sally, who were students at George Washington University. The Lymans, a youngish couple with a daughter Nat's age, completed the group.

It wasn't long before the water deepened, creeping over ankles and then knees.

"Hey!" Katy exclaimed as the cool liquid shocked her thighs. "If I'd known this was going to be a swimming party, I would have worn a bathing suit. How long will we be in the river?"

Paula turned to the young woman and answered in a voice loud enough so that everyone in the party could hear. "It's four miles to our destination. So we'll be wet for however long it takes to hike that distance."

Katy's eyebrows shot up. "You mean we're going to walk four miles upstream? Doesn't that mean we really will have to do some swimming?"

"Not at this time of year," Paula explained. "At least, not unless you want to. I've already scouted it and the water isn't more than waist-high except in some pockets and those are easy enough to skirt. This trip is going to be exactly what was advertised—a river splash. We're going to spend the day splashing our way up a quiet tributary and, I hope, learning something about its flora and fauna in the process."

After a few murmurs of anticipation, everyone settled down to doing exactly that. As the morning brightened and warmed, Paula was pleased to see that the hot summer weather was turning out to be absolutely perfect for the day she'd planned. The tree-shaded water flowing gently past was cool against knees and calves, and the warm sun that filtered through the leaves and onto everyone's shoulders made a pleasant contrast.

The morning flew by so agreeably that they arrived at the picnic spot she'd chosen before she even realized it was lunchtime. It was a sandy area near a water tower where there were flat rocks people could stretch out on. When the little band reached it, everyone was very glad to climb out of the river and open the waterproof plastic sacks in which they'd been instructed to bring their food.

For herself, Paula chose a place near the Lymans so that Nat and the Lymans' daughter, Sandy, could eat together. Ben and Katy perched on opposite ends of a big rock and conversed with the three women who made up the rest of the party.

The sun was now high in the cloudless sky, warming the rocks and streaking the bottle-green water with inlays of gold. Two brilliantly colored dragonflies pirouetted over the river's surface, and hidden in the woods, the cicadas droned a rhythmic background to the group's relaxed chatter.

Everyone did look relaxed, Paula thought, glancing around as she nibbled on a piece of cheese. Ben had just told a joke, and the three women sitting at his feet were all laughing up at him delightedly. Of course, that didn't surprise Paula. A man as charming as he was, was bound to have women eating out of his hand everywhere he went, she told herself.

Her gaze skimmed over his broad-shouldered figure. Like almost everyone else in the party, he was wearing cutoffs and a T-shirt. On Ben's lean, tightly muscled frame, the outfit took on a flair all its own, however. How, she wondered, would he look in a formal suit—or, alternatively, in a bathing suit? Or, for that matter, in nothing at all?

Just then his gaze caught hers again, and his blue eyes started to twinkle so devilishly that she had an irrational conviction he'd read her mind. Managing a weak smile, Paula took a gulp of juice from the plastic container in her hand and almost choked on it.

"Are you all right?" Katy asked, strolling over.

"Fine. How are you?" Paula cleared her throat and then moved over to make room for the eighteen-year-old. "Are you having a good time?"

"Great. When Dad first suggested this, I wasn't too sure. But I'm really glad we came." She sat down cross-legged next to Paula and grinned impishly. "For one thing," she whispered conspiratorially, "Sarah, Liz and Sally are having twice as much fun because he's here."

Paula followed the direction of Katy's glance. As they exchanged lighthearted banter with Ben, the three women's faces were aglow, and plain Sarah, the diffident schoolteacher, almost looked pretty.

"Your father is a very attractive man," Paula agreed.

"Yeah," Katy seconded. "But it's not just his sexy looks. He's great to be with. I'm really glad that he's finally decided to give up his job and settle down so that I can spend some time with him."

Curiously Paula studied Katy's unguarded face. The girl had reason to resent her absentee father—Ben had said so himself—but Paula could detect no sign of that. In fact, all morning the two Gallaghers had seemed to get along very well. "The only thing I know about your dad's job was that he spent a lot of time in South America," she said carefully.

Katy nodded and drained the last of her canned cola. "Secret, spy-type stuff. We never really knew what he was doing. Mom says he was born to be an adventurer and that he'll never give it up. But I disagree. Now that I've seen him here, I think he's ready to settle down." She shook her head. "I sure hope so, anyway. He's getting too old to play James Bond."

Paula wrinkled her brow. So Ben really had been working for the government when he'd been in South America. In what capacity, she wondered. But she couldn't ask his daughter and guessed that the girl didn't know. Already Katy had revealed more than she ought to, to a virtual stranger. Once more, Paula's thoughtful gaze strayed to the subject of their conversation.

Ben had gotten up to stand at the water's edge. As he looked out over the river, his feet were wide apart and his hands rested lightly on his hips. The man must be close to forty, and she'd already observed that the lines etched at the corners of his eyes and the deep grooves that ran from nose to mouth said he'd earned every one of those years. Could he really be happy to settle down in a quiet neighborhood to mow grass and run a small-time business? Paula just couldn't imagine it. She didn't voice her doubts to Katy, though. Why burst the girl's bubble?

After cleanup a few minutes later, everyone was back in the water for the last half of the trip. Now that they all knew what to expect, this part of the journey was even more enjoyable.

After they meandered along for a couple of hours, stopping now and then to paddle around in the small pools they occasionally discovered, they came upon a thicket of wild blackberries growing on the river's verge. Ben was the first to spot it.

"I think I see our afternoon snack ahead," he called, pointing at the prickly shrubs that bore the delicious fruit.

There were several whistles and a chorus of whoops as everyone realized what he was talking about. Then the scattered group, laughing and splashing, converged on the stretch of bushes to treat themselves to some of Mother Nature's bounty.

Loving wild blackberries, Paula was one of the first to station herself in front of them. She hadn't expected Ben to join her—he'd made such a point of keeping his daughter and her new friends company—but after a few minutes he came up alongside her.

"I feel as if I've somehow found my way back into the Garden of Eden," he commented. "This trip was a great idea. Did you think it up by yourself?"

"Yes," Paula admitted. As she filled her palm with fruit, she tried to ignore the sudden warmth his nearness produced. Just the sight of his sinewy forearms, their dusting of dark hair a sharp contrast against his bronze skin, made her stomach feel fluttery. "When I was a kid," she said, "I used to visit an aunt who had a house near a shallow river. I loved to play around in it, and I thought it would be nice to recreate that experience for county residents who were game to give it a try."

"So far this particular stretch of river has been perfect. It couldn't have been easy to find." He looked at her curiously.

"No. I poked around for weeks before I discovered just the right spot. Then, of course, I and someone else who works for the department had to take the walk to make sure it was okay."

As she reached for a berry, Ben's gaze remained fixed on her sun-dappled profile. He was picturing her out here alone, emerging from the water like a golden-haired river goddess. He'd once accused her of being unadventurous, but that wasn't true at all. In her own way she was an independent spirit. But she hadn't been completely alone, he reminded himself. "Who checked out the river with you?"

"Oh, it was Marty Henkel. A real nice young guy. You'll meet him this afternoon."

Ben struggled with a totally unreasonable stab of jealousy. Suddenly he wished that he could have been with her when she discovered this waterway. In fact, he wished he was alone with her right now, just the two of them in the sun together, feeling the cool water slide around their thighs and eating berries. He reached out and tugged her braid playfully. "I'm glad to see you still have this."

Paula slanted him a look. "I said I wouldn't cut it for now."

"Only for now?"

She paused to glare at him through her gold-tipped lashes. Almost instantly her expression melted into laughter. "Good heaven's, you can't expect me never to cut it!"

"Can't I? Hmmm, we'll see about that." His blue eyes gleaming, he popped a blackberry into his mouth and then glanced down at her cupped palm. "We have different blackberry-picking systems," he commented. "I'm eating as I go, but you're hoarding most of yours."

She nodded. "I'm greedy. For me, one berry at a time isn't good enough. My favorite thing is to fill my mouth with them." She glanced down at the glistening collection in her hand. "These are about ready to disappear."

He touched her shoulder and grinned. "That sounds like a great idea. But wait a second so I can join you."

While she watched in amusement, he quickly gathered a half dozen or so berries. Then, winking at her, he raised his hand to his mouth.

"Let's coordinate this effort. One, two, three—down the hatch!"

Laughing up at him, she crammed the blackberries she held into her open mouth and then closed her lips while she savored their rich, wild sweetness.

Ben had done the same. "Mmmm," he groaned as his teeth crushed the fruit.

"Mmmm," she murmured back.

Since she'd had far more berries than he, her mouth was still full when he lowered his head and whispered in her ear, "Sensualist." Then, while she gazed at him in astonishment, he lightly kissed her mouth, licking some of the sun-warmed juice from her lips and letting it meld with the juice on his.

Quickly Paula glanced around to make sure that none of the others had seen. But no one was looking in their direction. She shot Ben a reproving look. "You shouldn't have done that."

"No," he agreed with no visible sign of remorse. "But you have to admit it was very tempting. How often does a man get to kiss Eve in the Garden of Eden?"

Again, Paula felt herself going pink. "I'm not Eve," she muttered. Then turning away, she called to the others, "Hey, folks, if we're going to make it to the pickup spot before the sun goes down, we'd better get a move on."

There were a few good-humored grumbles, but everyone waded back into the river. Determined not to give Ben any more opportunities to disturb her equanimity, Paula fell in step between Liz and Katy, who were talking animatedly about student life at GWU.

From that point on, almost everyone seemed to divide into groups of twos and threes. The children were as lively as ever, but the Lymans, who'd preferred their own company for most of the day, strolled hand in hand through the water, talking in low tones. Ben, Paula noticed out of the corner of her eye, had joined Sally and Sarah. *Can't keep a good man down*, Paula thought. Whenever she'd looked at him during the day, he'd been effortlessly charming some wide-eyed female—including herself back at those berry bushes.

"How are we going to get back to the cars?" Katy asked, distracting Paula from thoughts of Ben.

"There's a bridge about a quarter of a mile up," she explained. "Marty Henkel, one of the guys from my department, will be waiting there with a station wagon. He'll take the drivers back to their cars and they'll return for their passengers." She glanced at her watch. "In fact, he's probably there now, wondering what on earth is keeping us so long." It was three o'clock, and Paula had expected to be finished by this time.

Katy laughed. "It was those berry bushes. After today I know what it must have been like to be a lotus-eater."

"Yes." Paula started to chuckle, but suddenly her amusement turned into a yelp of pain.

"What's wrong?"

Gingerly Paula tried to lift her right foot. "Something sharp just went right through the sole of my tennis shoe."

Whatever the thing was, it was big and it was keeping her shoe in the river. With only one foot to stand on in the moving water and with her other foot throbbing with pain, Paula's balance was precarious. Suddenly she lost it altogether and toppled over so that she found herself sitting up to her chin in the river.

"What's going on?" Ben demanded, wading over. After Katy explained what had happened, he squatted in the water to investigate Paula's trapped foot.

"You've stepped on a log with a big nail protruding from it," he announced grimly. "I'm going to pull it out, but it's not going to feel good."

That was an understatement, Paula thought as she bit her lip until it bled. Her foot finally freed, she gasped with pain and was in no condition to protest when Ben scooped her up in his arms and carried her to shore. In the next instant he had her ruined tennis shoe off.

"I hope you've had tetanus shots," he said. "You've got a puncture wound in the ball of your foot."

"I've had shots." She opened her eyes and saw the rest of the party still standing around, looking concerned and uncomfortable. She couldn't allow her own misfortune to ruin their day. "Folks," she called out as cheerfully as she could, "there's a bridge about fifty yards on down the river. Someone from the department is waiting there to take you all to your cars. I'd appreciate it if you'd tell him I'll be along shortly."

For a moment they all seemed uncertain, but at Paula's urging, the party began once more to straggle down the river, Katy taking charge of Nat.

"Do you have a first aid kit?" Ben asked.

"Of course." Undoing the plastic bag tied to her belt, she handed him the kit and watched as he rummaged around inside for disinfectant. It was going to sting, she thought, closing her eyes once more. This was exactly the sort of accident she'd most feared when she'd planned the trip. But when she and Marty had scouted this stretch of the river, it had really seemed clean. That submerged log had obviously escaped her explorations. She was just awfully glad that it had attacked her and no one else.

Paula braced herself, expecting at any moment to feel the burning antiseptic on her raw wound, but the sensation she suddenly found herself experiencing wasn't at all what she'd been trying to prepare for and her eyes flew open. While his palm cradled her heel and ankle, Ben's lips were pressed against the ball of her foot, sucking gently.

"What are you doing!"

He ignored her and didn't lift his lips until he was good and ready. Then, wiping his mouth on his sleeve, he explained, "I'm making it bleed. That's what you're supposed to do with puncture wounds, you know."

Paula did know. But when he put his cool lips against her flesh once more, she was too flustered to say so. All she could do was stare down at the top of his bent head. It was as if she were seeing him through a magnifying glass—the way the individual strands of crisp silver hair waved over the top of his ears, the dark, straight bars of his eyebrows and the lashes screening his gaze below his half-closed lids. Her gaze seemed to record the texture of his tan skin, the faint beginnings of a beard just visible below his cheeks and the shape of his mouth where he touched her. She felt the gentle but persistent movement of his jaw and inhaled sharply.

"That's enough, don't you think?"

Slowly he drew back and looked up at her, his eyes still fenced behind his lowered lashes. "Is it?"

"You have blood on your lip." In the slow, deliberate movements of a somnambulist, she leaned forward and touched the tip of a forefinger to his mouth.

His finger traced the delicate structure of her heel and then the line of her arch. "I'll dress the wound now."

She nodded, no longer worried by the sting of the antiseptic. Indeed, she welcomed the brief, cleansing pain because it shook her out of the sensual heaviness his intimate ministrations had created deep within her.

When her foot was neatly bandaged and she tried to get up, he gently pushed her back. "No, you shouldn't walk on that yet."

"But," she objected, "how will I get back to the bridge?"

"Simple. I'll carry you."

Paula opened her mouth. Then she shut it. There was no use putting up a fight. She couldn't get her foot back in her shoe, and it would be almost impossible to hobble along the rocky uneven riverbank. The alternative, wading through muddy knee-deep water, would be unpleasant and possibly dangerous. She certainly didn't need to take any more chances on getting an infection. Allowing Ben to scoop her up into his strong arms was the most sensible thing to do.

But when he cradled her against his chest, there was nothing sensible about the way it felt. His arms were like steel, and being held captive in them, with her head resting against his shoulder and the strong steady thrum of his heart in her ear, felt wildly, deliciously wicked.

"Are you sure you can carry me all that way? I'm no lightweight," she said in what she hoped was a level tone.

"My dear, you're as light as a feather. Even if you weren't, I assure you I wouldn't mind. It feels good to have a river nymph in my arms."

Paula's gurgle was appropriately watery. "I don't think nymphs step on nails. And you're flirting again."

He was, he admitted inwardly, but it was all in a good cause. Paula was bound to be in pain from that puncture wound and needed distracting. Aloud, he said, "Even goddesses occasionally put a foot wrong. You're allowed."

She tipped her head up so that she was gazing at the underside of his chin. How many men looked good from that angle, especially when they were beginning to need a shave? Not many, she guessed—but he did. "I'm allowed to step on nails?"

Suddenly his blue eyes, clear and bright, were gazing directly into hers. "No," he murmured. "I meant that you're allowed to live a little dangerously. Want to take a few chances with me?"

"What kind of chances?"

"I don't know. Let's put our heads together so we can think about it." Winking, he bent his head and blew in her ear.

Giggling, Paula batted her eyes at him. "You're really terrible, you know that?"

"Yes, but don't tell me you're not enjoying it. When you stepped on that damn nail, you went as white as a sheet. But now you've got rosy cheeks. I like them," he teased. "I just wish you'd give me a chance to see a little more of that gorgeous rosy skin."

Paula was still struggling for a reply to that outrageous sally when she realized that they'd arrived at the bridge. Ben left the river and climbed up the steep incline to the road. Pressed against his chest, with her arms around his neck, she was in a good position to monitor his physical condition. He must run marathons in his spare time, she speculated. The grassy slope that he was walking up without apparent effort wasn't exactly Mount Everest, but the man had a 120-pound weight in his arms that he'd just toted fifty yards through water. When he reached the road he wasn't even breathing hard, and his heart had quickened only slightly.

She certainly couldn't say the same for hers. It was beating double-time—and not because she'd exerted herself physically.

He'd just gently set her down, when the recreation department's one and only van, piloted by a grinning Marty Henkel, pulled up. Narrowing his eyes, Ben surveyed the vehicle's driver and then heaved an almost audible sigh of relief. The round-faced, good-natured-looking young man at the wheel was not competition.

Turning back to Paula with a smile, Ben said, "I'll drive your camper back to Parcel Court, and after I've dropped you off, I'll go up to the carryout at Martin Square and pick up some chow. That foot is probably already hurting like hell. You're not going to feel like fixing dinner."

"Thanks," she agreed gratefully. Now that she was no longer in his arms, the adrenaline that had been keeping her going suddenly deserted her. She was overwhelmed with exhaustion, and her wound was throbbing badly. All she wanted to do was sleep. But that didn't mean Nat wouldn't expect to be fed.

True to his word, after Ben chauffeured them back to Paula's house in the van and left her resting comfortably on the couch in the family room, he and Katy went off to do something about dinner. But an hour later, when the food arrived, it was Katy who brought it and Ben was nowhere in sight.

"Dad sends his apologies," Katy explained as she unpacked a bag full of sandwiches and milk shakes and set them on the kitchen counter. "When we got back to the house, there was a call on his answering machine. Some emergency that he had to go rushing off to Washington to attend to."

"When will he be back?" Nat demanded as he zeroed in on one of the chocolate shakes.

Ben's daughter shrugged and made a face. "He didn't know. But I hope to God this doesn't mean he's back to his old tricks," she said under her breath.

Nat paid no attention to the muttered words, but Paula had heard, and as she accepted the sandwich that Katy walked over to the couch to offer, there was a worried look in her eyes.

5

AT TEN THE NEXT MORNING, Ben dialed Paula's number. Since he'd been up all night brainstorming with Phil Walcutt and his men about the San Cristo situation, he was exhausted. Nevertheless, when he heard Paula's voice on the other end of the line, he smiled and his weary eyes brightened.

"I didn't wake you, did I?"

"No." She sounded surprised and, as usual, a little on her guard. Still, he had the feeling she was glad to hear from him.

"How's the foot?"

"Better."

"Good. Listen, Paula, I want to apologize for doing a disappearing act last night."

"I was...I was worried about you. What happened? Is something wrong?"

Well, if the lady was worried, that was a good sign, wasn't it? He ran a hand over his chin, noting that he was badly in need of a shave. He wished he could explain to her why things like this were sometimes part of his job, but, of course, that was impossible. "No big deal," he told her. "But I am sorry I missed seeing you last night."

She laughed. "I wasn't anything wonderful to look at. But if you want to see me this afternoon, all you'll have to do is look out your window. I have big plans to hobble around and pull weeds in my flower beds."

Ruefully he shook his head. "I'm afraid I'm not going to be around for the next couple of days. But that's not what I called to tell you. My pet shop is about to start business, and this Friday I'm planning an open house. I've already invited Nat. Will you come, too?"

There was a brief pause and he tensed while he waited for her answer. "Of course, I'll come," she said.

Considering the night he'd just been through, it was amazing how good he suddenly felt. "Great. I'll see you there."

After hanging up, he turned to find Phil standing behind him, a grim expression on his lined face. "I've got some java for you old buddy," Phil said, proffering a cup of black coffee that looked strong enough to jolt a half-dead horse back to life.

"Give me a break," Ben muttered as he accepted the plastic mug. "You know I want out of active duty."

"I do know and I wish I could tap another man." Phil shrugged. "But you're the one with the experience and know-how for this job. The fact is we need you too badly right now for me to give you a break. Will you do this one last thing for the department? Afterward, I promise you'll be off the hook. I won't ask you for any more favors."

Ben's blue eyes clouded. "I can't give you a decision now," he finally said. "I'll have to think about it."

NAT'S SHOUT ROCKETED up the stairs. "Mom, Gram's here. Are you ready?"

"No, I am not ready!" Paula pulled a mint-green knit top over her head. As she pushed her arms through the sleeves, she heard the click of high heels on the stairs.

"That color suits you, dear, but why don't you wear your white skirt with it? Then you'd look as cool and delicious as a crème de menthe frappé."

"Looking like a frappé has never been an ambition of mine." Straightening her denim skirt, Paula turned her head in time to see her mother bustle through the bedroom door. "This is a pet shop open house we're going to, not a royal wedding," she added, eyeing the gigantic pink flowers on Lynn's silky, full-skirted frock.

"Oh, I know dear, but Nat's talked so much about this Mr. Gallagher. I want to make a good impression."

"For heaven's sake, Mother, you don't need to worry about the impression you make on my neighbors. Ben Gallagher is only renting. He probably won't be here for more than a few months."

Avoiding Lynn's bright, speculative gaze, Paula hurriedly pinned her hair up and dabbed on some lipstick. Then she rushed around the room, gathering her purse, car keys and sunglasses. She hadn't exactly been thrilled when Nat announced, "Gram says she'd like to come too so she can meet Ben. I told her, 'Sure.'" It didn't take a genius to figure out that when Lynn got a look at Ben Gallagher, her matchmaking antennae were going to shoot up about a mile.

When they arrived at the shopping center, the open house had been underway for a little over an hour. The grassy area in front of the pet shop had been transformed into a kind of minifair. Under a striped canopy, a small band performed old favorites. Nearby, a clown capered about, amusing the children and giving away bright red balloons that read "Have you hugged your tropical fish today?"

Directly in front of the shop's display window was a booth where free beer for the adults and soda pop for the kids was being dispensed. At another stand, set a little distance away, ice-cream bars and tickets on chances for half-hourly drawings on free goldfish were being given out. Colored streamers festooned the freshly painted sign above the shop that read Gallagher's Tropical Fish.

In the midst of all this gaiety, Ben was standing in front of his new place of business, shaking hands with a line of customers. Though she knew he'd gotten back from his mysterious errand a couple of days earlier, this was the first time she'd had a good look at him since the previous weekend. He was, Paula noted, wearing safari pants and an open-necked cream silk shirt that emphasized his virile good looks, and he didn't appear the worse for wear. Whatever he'd been up to hadn't done him any harm.

"Goodness, this is quite a show," Lynn said. "I really hadn't expected anything so elaborate." She was looking around with a slightly bedazzled expression on her prettily rouged and powdered face. Suddenly her gaze honed in on Ben and became sharp as the needle nose on a heat-seeking missile. "That tall, silver-haired man in the doorway isn't Mr. Gallagher by any chance?"

The truth was not to be denied. Nat had already broken away and was skipping toward Ben, gleefully shouting his name.

Lynn arched an eyebrow and stared at her daughter critically. "You said he looked middle-aged."

"Well, he does have gray hair."

"So does Paul Newman."

"I didn't say he was ugly," muttered Paula.

Ignoring this puny defense, Lynn made a beeline for the man in question, her hand outstretched, her eyes sparkling with anticipation and a smile curling her lips.

Now I'm in for it, Paula thought, following her mother.

"Mr. Gallagher," Lynn sang out as she zeroed in on her quarry. "I'm Nat's grandmother, and I'm so charmed to meet you at last."

For a split second Ben looked startled. Then, over the top of Lynn's head, his eye caught Paula's and comprehension dawned. Shifting his blue gaze back to the tiny curvaceous older woman with the outstretched hand, he took it and favored her with his most beguiling smile. "You must be Paula's mother. Obviously, beauty runs in the family."

Lynn beamed. "Oh, aren't you nice! But I'm afraid my daughter takes after her father, not me. My husband was a tall, handsome devil, almost as handsome as you are."

Shuddering, Paula slipped past and found sanctuary in the pet shop. It was staffed by an assistant Ben had hired. After the young man had introduced himself as "Lou" and she'd shaken his hand, Paula looked around appreciatively. When Ben had described his color scheme to her, she'd been doubtful. But the freshly painted blue and green walls really did work. After the heat and glare of the searchlight sun outside, the shop was a peaceful haven. Glimmering in the muted light, the many tanks that filled the room gave the place the feel of an underwater cave.

Looking back over her shoulder, Paula saw that on the other side of the shop's glass door, her mother and Ben were still mixing introductions with compliments. Lynn had the same idiotic look on her face that most women seemed to get around Ben Gallagher. Tearing her gaze from the undignified sight, Paula started to walk around, admiring the fish. In one backlighted tank, zebra danios schooled together like bits of black and orange confetti. In another, neon tetras darted about in an erratic dance that made her think of aquatic fireflies. But Paula couldn't stay inside the shop forever. Turning from a container full of rainbow guppies, she stole another glance at the door. Ben was just coming through it.

"There you are," he said as he crossed to her side. "Your mother was wondering where you'd got to."

"I doubt that she was seriously concerned. She was much too busy drooling over you to worry about me."

"Your mother is charming."

"Well, she's certainly charmed by you. Where's Katy?"

"In Washington. She's enrolled in a special four-week summer school course. She's got a room in the dorm, so she won't be up here except occasionally on weekends."

"I'm sorry to hear that. You'll miss her, won't you?"

"Yes, but she has her own life to live, and I'll still get to see her. We're having lunch together next week." As Paula moved toward the door, he matched steps with her. "I notice you're hardly limping. How's the foot?"

"Fine. You missed your calling. You should have been a doctor."

"Medicinal urges only come to me in special circumstances and—" he winked "—with special patients."

Though she smiled at the compliment, the sideways glance she shot him was speculative. What had he been doing earlier this week? Did the emergency Katy said he'd been called away on have something to do with this mysterious South American connection of his? She wanted to ask, but of course, she couldn't.

Once outside, they both paused to take in the people enjoying themselves on the grassy expanse in front of the shop.

"This is quite a bash," Paula complimented him. "The clown is wonderful."

"There's a magician coming at three. I wanted to have pony rides for the little ones, but the mall management balked at the idea."

Paula laughed. "I should think so. Pony droppings are probably not their idea of landscaping." She gazed up at him curiously. What a surprising man he was. Who would have thought he'd go to so much trouble and expense to entertain the children in the neighborhood? But she could see from the expression on his face that he was really enjoying himself.

Suddenly he looked down at her empty hands. "Aren't you going to have something to eat?"

"I'll get a drink in a few minutes, but ice cream would spoil my dinner."

Just then one of the many youngsters who'd been clustered around the ice-cream stand ran up and tapped Ben on the elbow. "Mr. Gallagher, it's time for a goldfish drawing!"

Ben glanced at his watch. "So it is." His eyes twinkled at Paula. "Excuse me, I have a serious duty to perform. We'll continue this discussion later."

After he'd disappeared into the crowd Paula decided that, even though she didn't much like beer, she was thirsty enough to drink some and got herself a cupful. Sipping it, she scanned the crowd. She'd just spotted her mother and Nat eating ice cream and listening to the band when she was unpleasantly distracted by the cloying smell of hair spray and an all too familiar voice.

"Well, isn't this just something? Can you believe this?"

Resignedly Paula turned. It was Bernadette. Her hair stiffly bouffant despite the wilting heat, she was standing less than a foot away, holding a beer in one hand and a half-eaten ice-cream bar in the other.

"I'm not sure what you mean."

"I mean this . . . this display that our new neighbor is putting on." Bernadette gestured with the ice cream. "Now, I ask you, can you imagine what all this must be costing?"

"You mean the food and entertainment?" Paula's brow began to pucker. "A good bit, I suppose. You have to admit, it's awfully nice of the man to put himself out this way."

"Nice?" Bernadette shook her head darkly. "I don't think 'nice' has anything to do with it. Take my word, that Gallagher is a smart cookie. He's doing all this for a reason."

"To earn goodwill. That's the usual reason for an open house, isn't it?"

But Bernadette had her own theories. "He'd have to sell an oceanful of goldfish to pay for all this." Eyes narrowed, she pushed the last of her ice cream through her bright red lips and washed it down with a long swig of beer. "I think it's all a smoke screen—a ploy to make people around here like him so he can get away with murder."

"Murder!" Paula stared at her neighbor. She'd always wondered if Bernadette was playing with a full deck. Now she wondered if that deck wasn't loaded with jokers.

"I told you, that pet shop is just a front. Something else is going on, take my word."

Paula had no intention of taking Bernadette Carstairs's word for anything and controlled the impulse to say so only by biting her tongue. "Excuse me," she finally got out. "I think Nat is looking for me."

Actually Nat was happily downing his third ice cream and watching the magician pull rainbow strings of handkerchiefs out of his sleeve. After Paula had tapped her son on the shoulder and warned him off having any more treats, she veered away in search of her mother. She soon spotted her. Delicately sipping from a cup of beer, Lynn was once more conversing animately with Ben.

Oh dear, Paula thought as she headed toward them. *I wonder what she's up to now.*

"Oh, there you are," Lynn cried when she picked out her tall, willowy daughter's blond head weaving purposefully through the crowd. "I've been looking for you."

Paula hadn't seen any indication of that, but she elected not to argue the point. "Mother, I think we'd better be going pretty soon. Nat's eaten so much ice cream and drunk so much soda pop that he's about to overflow."

Though both Ben and Lynn chuckled at her words, they had a conspiratorial look about them that made Paula wonder what they'd been discussing.

Ben checked his watch. "You don't have to rush off yet, do you? The party is scheduled to end at four o'clock, which means that what's left of the food will be packed up in fifteen minutes. Once it and the clown and magicians disappear, so will everyone else, and I'll be left here all by myself with nothing but warm beer and melting ice cream to keep me company."

Lynn clucked her tongue. "Oh, dear. Does that mean you'll have to clean this mess up by yourself?"

"'Fraid so." Ben managed to look both hangdog and angelically resigned.

Clouds of suspicion began to gather in Paula's mind. They rose up and became thunderheads when her mother turned toward her and said innocently, "We can't allow that, can we? I know that we talked about going out for pizza, but after all Nat's eaten here, I don't think pizza for dinner is a good idea. He was planning on spending the night at my place, anyway. I'll take him back there now and feed him something light. That will leave you free to stay and help this nice man out. You'll do that, won't you, dear?"

For a long moment, Paula was silent. She was asking herself what she could say. Something like, "No. I'm afraid to be alone with Ben Gallagher because I get turned on every time he's within eyeshot?" Or how about, "I'm like the man who can't walk and chew gum.

I can't help him clean up and protect my virtue at the same time."

But clearly Lynn had no interest in protecting her widowed daughter's virtue, so what Paula replied after the long pregnant pause was "Sure."

It was almost comical. Ben and Lynn both looked like the cat who ate the canary—Lynn, because she was hot on the son-in-law trail and Ben, because he was hot on another trail altogether. *This is ridiculous,* Paula told herself as she watched her mother go off in search of Nat. *My imagination is working overtime. I'm just going to perform a little neighborly good deed, that's all.*

Ben had been right about the crowd. As soon as the eats and entertainment started to disappear, so did the people. He'd been considerably less accurate about his help. Far from being on his own, he'd hired the two teenage girls who'd served the food to help clean up. Between the four of them, it wasn't long before the area in front of the shop looked as good as new.

"What are you going to do with all this beer and ice cream?" Paula asked after he'd paid the teenagers and sent them on their way.

"There's only a keg left. That I'll take home. As for the ice cream . . ." He shrugged. "Any suggestions?"

"Yes," Paula said. "First off, that ice is almost gone, so you need to get the cartons into a freezer. I have one in my garage that you can use. Second, there's an orphanage next to the Episcopal church on Trotter Road. If you'd like, I could take the ice cream over there tomorrow."

Ben looked at her approvingly. "That's a great idea. You're welcome to it all—on one condition," he added. "Let me fix dinner for you tonight."

Paula put her hands on her hips. "You mean you're using orphans for blackmail?"

"A desperate man will go to any length." Seeing her expression, he quickly amended that. "The ice cream is yours no matter what. I'd just like to spend the evening with you."

Maybe it was Bernadette's unkind words, maybe it was seeing Ben giving out goldfish to the kids that afternoon or maybe it was just because she wanted to, but somehow it wasn't in Paula's heart to refuse. "Okay, but I have a condition."

Beaming as if she'd just given him a much longed-for birthday present, Ben said, "What?"

"That we get this stuff home before it melts all over the grass."

Laughing, he agreed to that. A quarter of an hour later, after he'd filled her freezer, he took her hand and looked at her questioningly. "You're still coming for dinner, aren't you?"

Paula hesitated, then nodded.

"Six-thirty all right?"

"Six-thirty's fine."

He smiled and then saluted. "See you then."

Without looking back, Ben drove away. He was glad she couldn't see his face. He knew he was grinning from ear to ear. So the lady was finally going to give it a chance, he thought as he pulled into the garage. Pushing open the door that led directly into the kitchen, he crossed to the refrigerator and studied its contents. Several cans of beer, martini olives, cold cuts, cheese, pickles and a salad left over from last night—not exactly gourmet fare. He looked at the clock over the sink. There was just enough time to run back up to Martin Square and buy a decent steak. Decisively he retraced his steps to the garage and then to the shopping center.

As he went through the motions, stopping first at the supermarket, then at the bakery for French bread and the liquor store for something special in the way of a Bordeaux, his mind was on the evening ahead. Just what was he hoping would come of this, he asked himself. Well, of course, that was a stupid question. He knew perfectly well that he wanted to go to bed with Paula Kirk. He'd had that on his mind for a long time now.

But there was more. When she'd finally said yes to his dinner invitation, he'd felt like letting out a war whoop. It had been years since he'd experienced that sort of elation, and then it hadn't been over a woman. It had been when he'd saved a buddy's life during a dangerous mission. So why was his adrenaline pumping now as if he were about to attempt the most delicate and important strategic assault of his life? At his age it was damned disturbing to feel this way.

But that didn't change anything. As he drove home and hurried back into the kitchen, his brain was clicking away like a computer—planning, organizing, arranging. Tonight, he wanted everything to be right.

FRESH FROM THE SHOWER and clad only in a towel, Paula eyed her wardrobe anxiously. What did one wear on one's first dinner date in over twelve years? She studied her blue-and-white sundress. The temperature today had topped ninety-five degrees and it was still breathlessly warm outside. But might Ben interpret those spaghetti straps and bared shoulders as some kind of sexual come-on? Her gaze drifted to a white camp shirt. She could wear that with a summery skirt, and the outfit would be cool and yet conservative.

"The hell with it," Paula muttered under her breath. She yanked out the dress and tugged it over her head. It was hot outside, and a person had the right to be comfortable.

She already had on gold hoop earrings. So once the dress was in place, she only needed to spritz on cologne, twist her hair back up into a loose knot and step into white sandals. After she'd applied lipstick and blusher, she scrutinized herself in the mirror. *I look nice*, she thought. *But I also look scared.*

Turning, she headed toward the stairs. Why should she be scared, she asked herself as she locked the door behind her, looked both ways and then walked across the street. She was a mature woman, for God's sake. She was just having dinner with the man.

But when Ben opened the door, she knew that it was going to be more than dinner. She knew it from the warm gleam in his eyes as his gaze drifted over her face, her bare shoulders, the swell of her breasts beneath the cotton bodice of her dress.

It was obvious that, like her, he'd just showered. Tiny beads of moisture still clung to his silvery hair, which was now neatly brushed back from his forehead. A faint sheen bloomed on his tanned skin and the dark thatch of chest hair just visible below his open collar. He'd changed into a charcoal-gray shirt and lightweight slacks of a slightly paler hue. He looked wonderful!

"You look wonderful," he said, and once again she found herself smiling up into his eyes as if they shared a secret.

"So do you. And," she added when he'd led her inside, "so does your living room."

Nat had mentioned that Ben had purchased a "bunch of neat new furniture," but that didn't begin to describe the transformation. The room was now dominated by an L-shaped modular seating arrangement with channel-stitched details and an overall streamlined design that looked European. Its buff velvet upholstery went beautifully with the black-and-gold Oriental rug in front of it. Though Paula was no expert, she knew enough about furniture to be quite certain that both pieces were very costly. The thought was a little disturbing because it made her recall Bernadette and her absurd charge that Ben was really some sort of mobster. That was ridiculous of course. But clearly the man had money to burn.

There were other changes in the room—a cigarette table with a black marble top, a rosewood wall unit with brass fittings and interior lights. The latter contained a handsome collection of pre-Columbian pottery and sculpture. Paula walked toward it and stood, studying some of the pieces.

"These are very nice."

"Thanks. I picked them up over the years, but I never had any permanent place to display them. So they just stayed packed up in storage. It was a pleasure to finally be able to put them out."

"Well, they're very interesting." Her gaze was arrested by a squat figure whose posture and enormous breasts made it clear that she was a fertility goddess. Abruptly Paula turned away. "What's for dinner? Can I do anything to help?"

"You can make the salad while I put the steaks on the grill. But before we do that, why don't we sit outside? After today, I could use a gin and tonic and a bit of relaxation. How about you?"

Paula agreed and a few minutes later she sank into a white wicker chair and noted with relief that Ben's patio was surrounded by a six-foot privacy fence. She smiled as he emerged from the kitchen, carrying frosty gin and tonics and balancing a tray of crackers and cheese. While the light waned they sipped their drinks, nibbled and talked.

"Evenings are the best part of summers in Maryland," she observed, inhaling the scented air appreciatively.

"Ummm, yes," Ben agreed. "This is going to be a good night for catching night crawlers."

"Night crawlers!"

Ben grinned. "Why do females always have that reaction? Haven't you ever gone on a night crawler hunt?"

"No, I haven't."

"Then sometime I'll have to teach you how it's done."

Paula didn't expect that that would ever happen, but tongue in cheek, she was willing to go along with the idea. "There's an art to catching night crawlers?"

"Oh, yes." He swirled the ice in his glass. "Well," he amended, "I'm not sure whether it's an art or a science, a little of both maybe."

Intrigued, Paula choked back a laugh. "But you've got the technique down pat?"

Ben smiled modestly. "I'm pretty good at it, even if I do say so myself."

"Are you going to tell me how it's done?"

"And reveal my trade secrets?" He gazed at her with mock gravity, then leaned forward conspiratorially. "Well, maybe I'll let you in on some of the basics."

"I'm all ears."

"That's certainly not the way I would describe you," he shot back, his gaze resting ever so briefly on her breasts. But before she could begin to bridle at this bit of sensuous flirtation, he cheerfully began to outline the Ben Gallagher technique for snaring night crawlers.

"Since you catch them at night, the first thing you need is a flashlight," he explained sententiously.

"Naturally."

"But you have to be quick. They're light sensitive, so you have to grab them before they snap back into their lairs."

"That sounds simple enough."

"It may sound simple, but it's not. Night crawlers are very crafty. They always keep part of themselves hooked in their holes. That's where the art and science come in. You have to get them out without breaking them in half."

Paula put up a hand. "Stop right there. I don't think I'm cut out for this type of work."

"I was afraid you were going to say that," he allowed.

She listened with pleasure to the sound of his rich laughter. When it died down, she said demurely, "Ben, there's only one more piece of information I'd like to have on this subject. Why do night crawlers come out at night?"

"To meet other night crawlers. What else?"

Now her laughter joined his, and reaching across the table, they clinked glasses in a mock salute.

When she'd come here tonight Paula hadn't known exactly what to expect. Who would have thought that a discussion of the habits of night crawlers would put her at ease? She looked across at Ben and gently shook her head. Yet, despite his relaxed charm, she sensed that he wasn't really completely at ease. The day she'd first laid eyes on him, his lean, silvery good looks had made her think of a creature of the wild. Now that she knew him better, she was even more conscious of a coiled watchfulness in him, an undomesticated quality that set him apart from other men.

But along with that faintly uncivilized aura, there was something else about him tonight. It was, she realized after they finally sat down to dinner, his total concentration on her. While she made a salad and set the black-marble-and-glass table in the dining room, he grilled steaks and corn. The meal, complemented by a delicious red Bordeaux that had been breathing on the sideboard, was wonderful, but as Paula ate and talked, she was hardly aware of the food or of the several glasses of wine she was rather recklessly consuming.

It was because her consciousness was absorbed by Ben. His attention was fixed wholly on her, on pleasing her, on charming her, on making her smile and, most of all, on learning more about her. He asked her questions about everything—her job, her childhood, even her favorite subjects in high school and college.

"I didn't really get to take many college courses," she admitted as they carried the dinner dishes into the kitchen. "I met Tim when I was a freshman, and we were married by the time that year was out."

"It sounds like he bowled you over." Ben poured two cups of coffee and put them on a tray along with a pair of brandy glasses.

"He did," Paula said, following him back out to the living room and settling onto the deeply cushioned couch while Ben put the tray down on the glass coffee table in front of it. "He was very handsome and very bright, and he had an absolutely wonderful voice."

"I was told that he was a newscaster."

"Yes. He gave the six o'clock news on channel eight. I have video cassettes of him at home."

"Do you ever watch them?" Ben had bent to put several different bottles of liqueur down on the coffee table, but his blue gaze was fixed intently on her.

"Once, about a month after he died. But I haven't since."

"Too painful?"

"Yes." The admission hissed faintly from her lips. Actually, except for the tapes, there were very few mementos of her married life left in the house. The day following the funeral, she'd cleared the dialysis equipment out of the spare bedroom. After his kidney failure, it had kept Tim going for almost two years, but there were so many horrifying memories associated with those dials and tubes that she hated the sight of them.

When they were gone, she hadn't stopped. Like a mad thing, she'd rushed through all the rooms gath-

ering up shoes, clothing, golf clubs, trophies, ash-
trays, books and magazines. Loading it all into the back
of the camper, she'd driven to a Goodwill collection
center and donated the lot. Back home, she'd collapsed in a heap on her bed and stared at the ceiling in
dumb misery.

"Here, drink this."

Ben's deep voice recalled her to the present. He prof-
fered a glass half filled with a thick, dark gold liquid.
She could smell the pungent orange sweetness.

"How did you know I like Cointreau?"

"Instinct." He sat down next to her and raised his own
brandy glass to his lips. "I have another instinct. Paula,
why are you talking to me about your husband now?"

"Why?" She stared. "I don't know."

"Tell me something." Once again, Ben's whole concentration was fixed on her. "Did you date much in high
school?"

"No. I was skinny and flat chested until quite late in
my teen years. I was also rather shy and kind of a loner."

"Was Tim your first boyfriend?"

"Almost." She took an overlarge sip of the Cointreau and felt it burn thickly down the back of her
throat. Ben was sitting very close to her on the couch,
one arm resting on the back. With his other hand, he
once more lifted the brandy glass. But even as he
drained its contents, his crystal gaze remained riveted
to her. It was unnerving to have a lean gray wolf sitting
so close, taking her so seriously, as if he could see into
her head and read all her thoughts.

"You were awfully young and inexperienced when
you were married."

"Yes." She swallowed uncomfortably but was unable to tear her gaze from his.

"Since you've been widowed, you haven't remedied that situation. I'm the first man you've allowed anywhere near you, aren't I?"

"Yes," she admitted again. Now she knew what he was getting at. "I'm not a trembling virgin, afraid to be alone with a man," she protested faintly. "I *was* married for a decade, you know."

Despite her protest, Ben studied her with a new sympathy and awareness. Yes, she'd been married for a decade but to a husband who'd been almost as young and inexperienced as herself. And what had Paula's relationship been with Tim Kirk during his two-year illness? Most probably, it hadn't been sexual. That meant she was a mature woman at the peak of her beauty who hadn't really had a lover for years. No wonder she was skittish.

"Paula," he said gently, "are you nervous about what's happening between us? Is that what's wrong?"

Evening had long ago fallen, and except for the backlighted display cases on the wall unit behind the couch, the living room was dark. In the shadows Paula's eyes were suddenly enormous. "Maybe a little," she conceded. Then she added quickly, "I'm not sure what's happening between us."

"Attraction," he said in his deep voice. "We're attracted to each other. We're both loners, and though most of the time we like it that way, we're lonely sometimes, too. Now and then we need to reach out and touch another human being." As he spoke, his fingers, lighter than butterfly wings, stroked her cheek. Then he set down his brandy glass. "Even if it's only for a night, we need to give comfort and have it returned. That's what's happening between us, Paula."

6

PAULA COULDN'T ANSWER. Everything he'd said was true. It was as if he'd seen into her soul, seen her need and her fear. She'd lain alone in her bed staring dry-eyed through the darkness and wondering if she'd ever again feel the warmth of a man's arms, the closeness of a shared night. She didn't require it, she'd told herself. The risks were too great. But for the moment, as she met Ben's blue gaze, that wisdom was forgotten and an older, more compelling knowledge throbbed in her veins.

He had moved closer to her and reached out. Now his hands were on her hair, slowly removing the pins that kept it coiled on top of her head.

"I thought you said you weren't a trembling virgin."

"I'm not."

"You're trembling now. You're shaking like a leaf and I'm hardly touching you."

"That's because it's cold in here. You've got your air-conditioning turned up high."

"Then, as your host, it's my duty to warm you, isn't it?" Deliberately he removed the last pin, and her hair tumbled around her shoulders. Then, with equal deliberation, he wrapped his arms around her and drew her close. As his head bent toward hers, blocking out the light, she shut her eyes and waited. Since she'd already tasted Ben's kisses, she knew they were wonderful. For the rest—she'd wait and see.

He didn't disappoint her. When his lips took hers, it was with the same friendly persuasion he'd always shown. Her mouth opened, and he invaded it, teasing her tongue with his, playing little games that almost made her smile and definitely made her soften against him.

"This is nice," he whispered, drawing back slightly. "But you're still trembling."

"Am I?" Paula didn't think that was true, but she wasn't going to argue.

"Yes. Tell me where you're cold, so I can do something about it."

His eyes were teasing her, but somehow she managed to keep a straight face. "My shoulders."

"Yes, I've noticed those cold shoulders of yours," he drawled, laughter welling just beneath the rich surface of his voice. "You've given me more than my share, you know." His gaze drifted over the bare skin above the line of her bodice. "I can't account for the cause in the past. Tonight, I think it's those straps on your sundress." Carefully he brushed them down over her arms. "They interfere with your circulation."

The corners of her mouth quivered. "Oh, is that the problem?"

"Mmm, well maybe they need a little personal attention." With one hand against the small of her back and the other supporting her head, he tipped her slightly. Then, first smiling into her eyes as if to reassure her of his good intentions, he rubbed his cheek against the point of her shoulder and nipped lightly.

She giggled, and he laughed with her. "We have to stimulate those cold shoulders a bit," he explained, a devilish light in his eyes. "But you know what?"

"What?"

"Sometimes in difficult cases like this it's best to go directly to the heart of the matter." As he spoke his lips moved back to her throat and then down to the flesh just above her bodice.

Paula shivered, but this time it was definitely not from the cold. "What do you mean by that?" she questioned, aware that her voice had thickened.

"I mean that when a person needs to be warmed up it can be a good idea to concentrate on certain select spots." While his eyes looked into hers, one hand had gone to her back and slowly pulled down the zipper of her sundress.

There was nothing rushed about this smooth seduction. At each stage Ben waited for her to stop him. But Paula knew she wasn't going to.

As if he'd read her mind, he suddenly grinned. "I'm glad to see that you concur with my strategy."

"I have nothing but awe and admiration for your strategy."

Then she gasped. Ben had pressed her down into the soft cushions of the couch. His hand brushed the top of her loosened dress away and her breasts spilled free. As he looked down at them, his pupils dilating and his features going suddenly taut, she sobered. What until now had seemed like play was suddenly more serious. It wasn't just that she saw the changes in Ben's expression. She could feel the same thing happening within herself. As his gaze burned down, her breasts seemed to heat and swell. The nipples tingled, and she didn't need to look at them, only at Ben's shadowy countenance to know that they'd hardened into small pink nubs of desire.

"I knew your breasts would be beautiful," he said in a thickened voice. Then his mouth was on them, kissing, nuzzling, licking. His lips closed around a straining peak and he laved it with swirling motions of his tongue and then pulled gently. Through the velvet fog that descended over Paula's thought processes, she heard herself moan. The movements of Ben's lips had produced a knot of aching sensation that raced downward, settling unequivocally at the juncture of her thighs.

It had been a long time, but Paula recognized her body's brushfire reaction. She hadn't thought it could happen so quickly. Yet it had, and she knew there was no going back now.

Reaching up, she drew his head close. While his mouth remained at her sensitized breast, his hands pushed her dress farther down her torso, and she didn't even think of protesting. Behind her closed eyelids, colored lights flashed and flared. Cool, rich lavenders and velvety wine-reds intertwined, lacing themselves together with threads of gold.

The gold became incandescent, shimmering like strange, magical fire as Ben's hand moved against her bared skin. Then his fingers slipped inside her panties, and the gold began to twist in a sinuous dance, forming writhing shapes, each more fantastic and beautiful than the last.

He'd gone straight to her most sensitive secret. Her needs were no mystery to this lover. But far from resenting his knowledge, Paula rejoiced in it. At this moment she wanted nothing more than to be understood, to know fully and be fully known. Her thighs parted slightly, and she held him tight.

His hand never stopping, he raised his head and studied her. What he saw in the arch of her vulnerable throat, her parted lips, her tightly closed lids satisfied him, and a moment later, as she trembled and went rigid in his arms, he knew a satisfaction, a triumph that was as exciting as any other he'd ever experienced.

When, dazedly, she opened her eyes, it was to find his blazing into them.

"Paula, let me make love to you."

"Yes."

"But not here." Brushing her dress away completely so that she wore only her white silk bikini panties, he scooped her up into his arms and walked with her out of the room. She had been trembling earlier. Now, pressed against his chest, she realized it was he that quivered. His taut body was vibrating with excitement. The realization made her feel weak. Yet in another way, she felt strong, too. It was something to lie in the arms of a lover like this. The morning might bring regrets, but at the moment Paula was willing to pay the price.

One wall of Ben's bedroom was dominated by a hundred-gallon aquarium. It provided the only light, and for an instant or two, when he laid Paula down on the massive, strangely resilient bed opposite, she blinked in disorientation.

"A water bed?"

His gaze fixed on her, Ben was was rapidly stripping off his clothing. "For my bad back."

She thought she caught an apologetic note in his voice and had to smile. "I'll bet."

He smiled back and then undid his trousers and stepped free. "All right, I like water. You will, too."

She didn't answer. She was too busy taking in the sight of his body in the shifting light from the aquarium behind him. He could put on ten pounds and no one would notice, she thought. But she liked him the way he was—every flexed muscle clearly defined, his belly so flat that it was concave, his hips both sleek and tight, his legs long, hard and corded with muscle. Even in the muted illumination she could see the sharp contrast where his shorts protected his skin from the sun. He was very male—so much so that it made her shiver slightly—feeling her softness, her vulnerability underlined in comparison.

Naked, he stood for a moment. His body was a dark outline against the blue-green water. It sent out long tendrils of reflected light that shimmered and danced against the ceiling.

"Paula, you're a beautiful woman," he murmured. "I wonder if you know what it means to me to see you finally lying like that in my bed."

"You make it sound as if seducing me has been a long-term project." Her throat was dry, but she was determined to conduct herself like the adult she was—no coyness, no uncalled-for declarations. "It's really only been a few weeks. Have I held out so much longer than most of your other women?"

He came to her then, stretching his length out and taking her in his arms. "I don't want to talk about other women. There are no others in my mind now. And this isn't a seduction. You musn't think of it like that."

"Then how must I think of it?"

"As a consummation. Finally, after all this time, we've found each other. Now we're celebrating the fact."

She didn't know what he meant and was in no shape to sort it out, because she was in no condition to think at all. Ben's body was like a furnace. It threw off heat that raised her temperature, making the blood nearly simmer in her veins. At the same time she was vividly conscious of the cool, smooth coverlet beneath her, the unfamiliar buoyancy of the water bed that cradled her body. The sensual melange was heightened by the feel of Ben's warm hand lightly stroking her hair and then her breast. He kissed her forehead, his lips chaste and dry against her skin. His knowing hands continued to drift over her body, electrifying every spot they met.

"How do you like to be touched?" he whispered. "Show me."

She curled her hands around his shoulders, amazed at the steely muscle just beneath the masculine satin of his supple hide. "No, you're doing fine. Show me what you want."

"I want you to let me please you."

"But . . ."

"No, shhh, just let me please you." His lips found hers, silencing her protest while his hands continued their slow, rhythmic explorations. She sighed against his mouth, her fingers unconsciously testing the un-yielding muscle she still clenched. She was trying to steady herself, but it was a hopeless effort. Suddenly she felt as if she'd tumbled off the edge of a cliff.

"You like that, don't you?" he growled.

"Yes."

"And this?" Once more his head went to her breast, his lips tugging gently but sensuously on a swelling crown.

"Yes."

"And this." His thumb moved along the inside of her thigh, drawing a delicate pattern that clearly had an ultimate goal. A few heartbeats later he'd achieved it.

"Yes!" Paula's voice was a thin gasp.

"Let's see what else you like."

"Oh, Ben . . ."

"After tonight, you're not going to have many secrets. If we're to make up for lost time, I have to know everything about you. Everything."

While that alarming, exciting hand of his continued its play, his head moved down from her breast. He dropped slow, damp kisses on her rib cage, her smooth stomach. Then he moved lower yet.

Not even sure what he intended, but beginning to guess, Paula twined her fingers in his hair and tugged. The intimacy rapidly flowering between them seemed more than was right. But Ben, who was very sure of what he wanted, ignored her fluttering, voiceless objections. And very soon she was beyond protest. Her hands left his hair to once more grasp his shoulders, and she arched toward him. The pleasure fountaining deep inside her body was its own imperative and couldn't be denied.

When he felt her shudder beneath him and tasted her liquid warmth, Ben moved up beside her. "Now?" he whispered.

Still lost in sensation, Paula could hardly articulate the words. "Oh, y-yes!"

With one hand she feverishly stroked his back. With the other, she touched the smooth, adamant line of his hip, urging him toward her. Now she was as sure of what she wanted as he. But Ben held back a moment, turning away from her slightly. At first she was puzzled, but then gratitude flooded through her as she realized what he was doing. Precautions at this time of the month were probably unnecessary, but how considerate of him to take them without embarrassing her by asking.

As he positioned himself between her thighs, Paula moved her smooth calf up his hair-sprinkled one, then hooked it behind his knee and tilted her pelvis in age-old feminine invitation. With a groan of impatience, he moved to close with her. Her fingertips seemed to tingle with the electricity he generated, and as Paula's every pulsing nerve sensed his slow, compelling invasion, a primal vitality rippled through her.

For a long moment they were both still, savoring the satisfaction of their union. "Paula, this is so good." His voice was thick. "We fit so perfectly, so beautifully. Everything about you is beautiful." Abruptly he kissed her, not with the friendly persuasion he'd used before, but with a possession that was almost rough. His tongue appropriated her mouth, just as the rest of his body was staking an uncompromising claim. And as the kiss went on so that she was almost breathless beneath the force of it, she felt his strong fingers twine through her long hair.

In that split second Paula felt more desired, more prized than she ever had before in her life. Her arms wrapped themselves around Ben's muscled back, her fingers running in restless excitement up and down his smooth, tough hide. At the same time her knees pressed tight against his flanks, as if it were possible to cage his vibrant masculinity and receive more of him within herself. Sensing the welcome in her capitulation, he groaned his satisfaction and then, slowly but relentlessly, began to move. He was a strong, determined man, primed for control, tempered for endurance. As his rhythm increased but never faltered, she knew he would be there for her.

In the room's strange shimmering blue darkness, on the bed's buoyant, rippling surface, she was conscious of nothing but the fiery summons of Ben's driving motions. It was an imperious ultimatum that must be answered, and suddenly, joyfully, she knew it would be. A key seemed to twist inside a lock. She opened to him, and a dark barrier crashed soundlessly so that light could pour through. Every part of her body glowed with it, even the soles of her feet. Every cell was bathed in sunshine, every nerve suffused with radiance.

"Oh, Ben," she gasped.

But he'd already felt her tremulous release. At last, his hips churning feverishly, he took his own.

He collapsed against her, and her hair, spread fanlike on the pillow, was a scented curtain against his cheek.

"Paula," he murmured, "Paula."

She didn't know how to answer him. All she could do was stroke his back. It was damp from his exertions. Beneath his hair-matted chest she could feel perspiration on her breasts and her belly, too. But it was a good, healthy animal feeling. And suddenly that was exactly the way she felt—at one with herself and the world, like a creature who was gloriously, totally alive and whose every need had just been utterly satisfied. Enjoying the sensation of skin against skin and the ripple and cry of her own muscles and nerves, she stretched beneath him in languorous appreciation.

"Move against me like that now and you're inviting a return engagement," he growled in her ear.

She gave a husky laugh. "After that virtuoso performance, I think I'm safe."

Rolling to one side and taking her with him, he chuckled. "All right, you're probably safe for the next ten minutes, but you're a powerful temptation, lady. I wouldn't give it any longer than that."

He kissed her, and then with obvious regret, got up off the bed. A moment later she heard water running in the adjoining bathroom. While he was gone, Paula's eyes went to the aquarium opposite the bed. All during their lovemaking, she'd been dimly aware of it. Now she studied it with interest. It was by far the most beautiful she'd ever seen. That was partly, but not wholly, because of its large size. The aquarium dominated the entire wall, giving the effect that the bedroom opened onto an underwater landscape.

And what a landscape! Among the gently swaying ferns, giant silvery-white angels drifted about, their long trailing fins floating behind them, making Paula think of misty wedding veils. Like animated blood-red poppies, cardinal tetras bloomed. An electric-blue Siamese fighting fish darted among them, flourishing its imposing dorsals as if they were the lush plumage of some impossible tropical bird.

"Your aquarium is very beautiful," Paula murmured when Ben returned and once more stretched himself out at her side.

"Thanks. I like looking at it before I go to sleep. Luckily, this house is built on a slab. Otherwise, I wouldn't be able to put so much weight on the floor." But he didn't want to talk about fish. Capturing her cheek, he turned her face toward his. "Paula, you're a beautiful lover."

She answered without artifice. "No, you're the expert. I just lay there gasping while you played me like a violin. Compared to you, I'm a novice."

"It's not difficult to make beautiful music on a Stradivarious."

"Not difficult if you're an accomplished musician."

Slightly troubled by her neutral, matter-of-fact tone, he studied her. She looked so lovely with her hair spread around her. He could gaze at her, run his hands over her for hours. "Paula, I'll be forty in a couple of months. Does it bother you that over the years I've learned something about women?"

"No, of course not." She laughed at him lightly. "I'm glad...grateful. Because of you, tonight I've learned something about myself. I didn't know that I could...that it could be so—"

"Fine?" Not quite meeting his eyes, she nodded, and he felt a rush of pleasure at her shy acknowledgment. "I'll tell you something. Until tonight, I didn't know that myself."

"What?" She laughed again. "Listen, now that I think about it, maybe it wasn't just your expertise. Maybe this sinful bed of yours had something to do with it. It's very—" she paused, giving him an impish look "—pneumatic."

"Pneumatic!" Ben roared and then reached over and started to tickle her. "I'll pneumatic you. Shall I throw you onto the hard floor and make love to you there so you can compare?"

Wriggling and laughing, she shook her head. "No, I think I'd rather stay where I am."

The tickling slowed and became a long caress. The light from the aquarium played over Paula in a way that made him remember how she'd looked in the river. So he'd finally lured a river goddess to his bed. The sight of her—her full, pouting breasts, her smooth, lightly curved hips, the downy secret between her silken thighs—had its inevitable effect. Once more, heat rushed to his loins. Wordlessly he gathered her into his arms, kissed her soft mouth with thorough possession and then pressed her into the buoyant mattress.

The second time was different from the first, slower, more languorous. When it was over, Paula, totally sated, curled her body against Ben's and drifted off to sleep. It was a while before he did the same. Instead, still cradling her in one arm, he managed to lever himself up against the headboard without disturbing her. Then he reached over to the bedside table and lighted a cigarette one-handed.

A year earlier he'd virtually given up smoking and these days didn't allow himself the luxury of a cigarette very often, but tonight the indulgence seemed called for. Tonight was special, very special indeed. He glanced down at Paula. Her head rested partly on the pillow, partly in the crook of his arm, her hair splayed across it. He'd drawn the sheet up around them so that now it covered his waist and the tops of her breasts. But even as he watched, she moved in her slumber so that the sheet slipped and one pink nipple peeked out. The effect on him was instantaneous. He desired her yet again. But she was sleeping so sweetly that he didn't have the heart to wake her.

Instead of doing what he wanted, he drew deeply on his cigarette and watched the smoke drift toward the ceiling. While he willed his body to settle down, a million thoughts and feelings tumbled together. As he'd already told Paula, he was nearly forty. There'd been other nights of passion—a lot of them. Briefly he recalled some of the many women who'd lain in his arms. Then he looked down at the woman next to him and forgot the others. They weren't important anymore. He knew what he wanted now. It was as clear as the water in the aquarium, and as he contemplated that fact, an enormous satisfaction welled within him.

7

PAULA FLOATED on a warm, gentle sea. It was lit by sunshine, rays of which bathed her face in golden light. The sensation was so pleasant that the corners of her mouth lifted as she slowly opened her eyes. But the creature she saw staring at her wiped away the smile. She froze and then started to blink rapidly.

It was a fish. In fact, there were several giving her the eye. They were peering out of Ben Gallagher's mammoth tank, as though disdainfully curious about the odd inhabitants of the world beyond their own.

Abruptly she swung her head to the left, an action that caused a disconcerting undulating motion in the bed in which she'd spent the night. But that wasn't half as disturbing as seeing Ben Gallagher's naked back next to her. Vividly Paula recalled the events of the evening before, and as she reviewed what had happened between herself and this man, her cheeks began to grow warm.

Slowly her gaze traveled from the thick head of tangled silver hair that waved around his well-shaped ears and grew low on his nape. There were freckles on his broad shoulders. His tan was so deep that they were almost invisible, but up close this way, with the morning sun coming through the window, she could just make them out. Sometime in the night he'd kicked off the sheet, so she had an unobstructed view of the line at his waist where his tan ended. Below it, skin of a much paler hue covered buttocks that were small and flat, a sharp contrast to the broad bronze shoulders flaring up from his narrow waist. She'd cradled that waist between her thighs last night. The memory produced a dryness in her mouth and a familiar ache.

Automatically one of her hands reached out, but after it hovered over him a moment, she snatched it back. Paula knew that Ben would make love to her again if she wakened him. He would turn toward her, enfold her in his arms, and before long she'd be awash in the pleasures he'd shown her during the night.

But what would that accomplish? Paula stared up at the ceiling and tried to think. Last night had possessed its own logic, but the clear light of day called for wisdom that was a bit more conventional. Did she want to become a Ben Gallagher addict? Did she want this to be the beginning of an ongoing affair? As she contemplated what that would mean, her stomach clenched.

Frowning, she pictured herself sneaking across the street when Nat was away, or even when he was just asleep. Praying that no one would see her, she'd have to come home again in the middle of the night or at dawn and, for her son's sake, resume her squeaky clean image.

That simply wasn't a scenario with which she could live. Suddenly there was a lump in Paula's throat she couldn't swallow. She had no regrets about last night—or at least none that she could take very seriously. She was an adult woman with adult needs who was now in many ways alone in the world. Surely after almost two years of widowhood, she'd had the right to be swept away in a moment of passion and accept temporary solace. But this sort of thing couldn't go on—not if she was going to be a good mother to Nat and maintain her self-respect.

Casting one last lingering and rueful glance at Ben's back, she turned away and rolled toward the edge of the rosewood bed frame. But that started up another rippling undulation. Once a female had been lured onto this supersensitive, king-size mattress of Ben Gallagher's, she wasn't going to get off unobtrusively, Paula reflected.

Shrugging, she clutched the loose sheet around her breasts, levered herself off the edge and sprang as lightly as possible onto the carpet. The bed heaved like a wind-tossed sea. But Ben was apparently used to wave action. Though he shifted slightly, he didn't open his eyes and his breathing remained slow and steady. A faint smile hovering around her lips, Paula gave him a last admiring look. The poor man must be exhausted, she thought. Not surprising when she considered the energy he'd expended on her the night before.

Wrapping the sheet around her like a toga, she turned and made her way out of the bedroom. She padded down the hall toward the living room, where she remembered leaving her clothes. The sight that greeted her made her rub a dismayed hand across her forehead. Appropriately enough, the area around Ben's modular couch looked like the aftermath of a suburban debauch. Her shoes lay tipped helter-skelter on the rug. The sundress she'd debated wearing, afraid he might interpret it as a come-on, dangled over the edge of the sofa cushions in a tangle. The pins Ben had removed from her hair were scattered in disarray.

The dress had been designed to be worn without a bra, so the only thing missing was her panties. In a gesture of pure embarrassment, Paula put her hands up to the top of her head and clutched at her loose hair. They were somewhere in Ben's sybaritic bedroom. In case he woke up, she didn't really want to go back there and root around for them. On the other hand she wasn't exactly crazy about leaving her underpants behind, either.

Gritting her teeth and letting the sheet drop, Paula started to uncrumple her dress and yank it over her head. Oh, well, she told herself as she stepped into her shoes and gathered up her hairpins, the man must be used to this sort of thing. The indications were that he'd had a parade of women in and out of his bedroom. Surely he would find an unobtrusive way of returning her underwear. Unless, of course, he kept such items as trophies. For all she knew, he had a bronzed collection somewhere.

Then she pulled herself up short. This situation had her so much off balance that she wasn't thinking straight. Ben might be experienced, but he wasn't some kind of leering gigolo. He was an intelligent, sensitive man who'd treated her to an unforgettable night. It wasn't right to just sneak away without a word.

Thoughtfully she glanced in the direction of the hall. The fact remained that she wasn't quite ready to face him again and didn't want to wake him up. Maybe she could just leave a note. Her gaze fell upon the wall unit behind the couch. It had what looked like a fold-down writing desk. Maybe if she opened it, she would find paper and something with which to scribble a few words.

She'd guessed right. There was notepaper behind the rosewood panel. But as Paula rummaged for it, her eye fell on a yellow legal pad covered with thick, angular strokes. That must be Ben's handwriting, she thought, peering at the pad more closely. It was obviously a report of some kind that he'd been working on. Several pages were filled. But though the letters were clearly formed, the words were unreadable. Paula cocked her head and realized that she couldn't understand what Ben had written because it wasn't in English. Arrested, she lifted the pad and stared at it curiously. She'd had a year of Spanish in high school and recognized the language. But tenth grade had been a long time ago. She couldn't make head or tail of the sentences.

There was, however, one capitalized phrase that stood out from the text, and it was repeated several times. *El Ejercito de los Puños*. Roughly, that translated as, "The Army of the Fists." Paula frowned. She'd heard that term somewhere before—on the six o'clock news, she suddenly realized. Weren't the *Puños* the counterrevolutionaries who were fighting a guerrilla war against the newly formed junta in San Cristo? She was aware that the small but strategically located Central American country had been torn by continual political upheavals over the last decade, many of them bloody. Was Ben somehow involved in all that?

Quickly replacing the yellow pad, Paula shut the desk and backed away from it. The idea of leaving him a note had been wiped from her head. All she could think of now was a speedy departure and a long hot shower in the safety of her own bathroom. Maybe Bernadette was actually right, she thought as she headed for the front door. There were all kinds of stories about San Cristo—gun running, the drug trade. Maybe that pet shop really was a front. In the last couple of weeks Ben Gallagher had spent a small fortune on the luxurious furnishings in this house. And what about the costly bash he'd thrown yesterday at the shopping center? As Bernadette had nastily pointed out, he obviously hadn't done these things on money he'd made from selling goldfish.

Her fingers on the doorknob, Paula once again pulled herself up short. She had no reason to distrust Ben and every reason not to take Bernadette Carstairs seriously—except when it came to being the subject of the woman's gossip. Paula yanked her hand back as though the knob were on fire. Where were her brains? All she needed was to be spotted emerging from a sexy bachelor's front door at breakfast time. The tom-toms would start to beat before she even made it across the street.

Pivoting, she hurried to the patio door, pushed it open and peered out. The only tricky thing would be slipping from behind Ben's privacy fence and onto the grass without being seen. Once she'd made it to the sidewalk, she could walk around the corner, and if she were observed, it would just look as if she'd taken a morning stroll. Thank goodness she'd worn a simple sundress last night and not some sort of slinky concoction that was obviously meant for evening.

Five minutes later Paula made it into her own side entrance and collapsed against the kitchen counter. "Whew!" she said aloud. Though it had taken only a few seconds, the trip across the street had seemed interminable, and during the whole of it, she'd been acutely conscious she wore nothing beneath her demure little sundress.

Pushing herself away from the sink, she went to the mirror next to the bookcase in the family room and then groaned. She'd been so eager to pull on her dress and get out of Ben's house that she hadn't given much thought to the rest of her appearance. Now she saw that her hair was tangled and that her lips were still swollen from last night's lingering kisses.

Refusing to think about those kisses or the passion she and Ben had shared, she shook her head in dismay and turned to rush up the stairs. Nights of wild abandon were fine, she thought as she stepped under the spray and started to vigorously scrub her body with her lathered washcloth, but mornings after were the pits. She jerked off the taps and felt around for her yellow terry cover-up. She was too old for this sort of thing. Maybe it was all right for movie stars and libidinous single ladies who lived in anonymous high-rise apartments, but it wouldn't do for someone like her.

When Paula walked out of the bathroom, the phone was ringing. She stared at it for a moment and then stepped forward and picked the thing up. It might be Lynn calling about Nat. But it wasn't. It was Ben.

"Why did you leave without saying a word? I thought we were going to have breakfast together." He sounded aggrieved, almost as if he were hurt and trying not to let it show. At the sound of his deep baritone, she felt some of her resolve melt and a helpless tingling start up in the area of her breasts.

"I . . . I didn't want to wake you."

He dismissed that gruffly. "You can wake me anytime and you know it. Come on back. I picked up croissants and fresh strawberries when I shopped for dinner. We can have those on the patio with our coffee."

It was a seductive picture, but she forced herself to ignore it and to concentrate on the implications of his invitation. So yesterday he'd planned on her spending the night and shopped accordingly. The realization stiffened her spine a bit. "I can't come back to your house, Ben. Just trying to make it back to my house this morning without looking so guilty that everyone on the street would guess how I'd spent the night was a major trauma. My stomach is still tied in knots. I'm not up to this sort of thing."

"What do you mean?"

Paula took a deep breath. "I'm not a swinging single."

"You're as single as I am."

"But I can't lead that kind of life. I have a young son and a reputation to consider. I can't carry on an affair with a neighbor."

"Paula, surely that's not the way you think of me. I'm not merely a 'neighbor.' I'm Ben, the man you made love with last night. Just what exactly is it that you're telling me?"

Again, there was a painful lump in her throat, but she knew what she had to say. "Last night was wonderful, and I'll never forget it. But it can't happen again. I'm not coming across the street to your house anymore. For obvious reasons, I can't invite you to mine."

There was a long silence and then the phone clicked. Paula took the receiver away from her ear and stared at it. He'd hung up on her. What did that mean, she wondered.

It wasn't long before she found out. On the way downstairs to fix herself a cup of coffee and take an aspirin for the headache that was now beginning to pound at her temples, she suddenly heard steady hammering from the direction of the sliding glass door at the back of the house. A worried look on her face, she ran into the family room and then stopped short. Barefoot, dressed only in cutoffs, Ben was standing on the other side of the glass scowling at her. In one balled fist he held a crumpled bit of white silk. So much for being unobtrusive!

"Oh, my God!" Paula exclaimed. She rushed to the door and pushed it open a crack. "What are you doing?" she snapped. "Did anyone see you walk over here dressed like that?"

Eyeing her irritably, he ignored the question and thrust her underwear at her. "I want to talk to you, and I'm not going to do it on the phone."

"Well, I don't want to talk to you, not here, not now." Very ruffled, Paula took her panties and stuck them deep in her pockets. "I told you—"

"You're afraid the neighbors might gossip," Ben completed the thought. His expression was caustic. "Well, if you don't let me in, I'll put my fist through this damn glass. That will really give the neighborhood something to jabber about."

Instantly Paula slid the barrier back and stood aside. "This is ridiculous!" she muttered through her teeth.

"You're absolutely right. What you told me over the phone made no sense whatsoever." While Ben turned to confront her, Paula made a business of pushing the glass closed behind him.

"I tried to explain it to you."

He snorted. "What you said was that you weren't 'up to this sort of thing,' as if I'd invited you to compete in a Hula-Hoop marathon." He reached out and seized her wrist. "Paula, why are you saying things like that to me? Why are you behaving this way?"

"What way?" Her tone was defensive and she refused to look directly at him. Ben's steely blue eyes, however, were boring straight into her.

"As though last night wasn't special. As if it was just some sort of strictly carnal, one-night stand that didn't mean much to either of us."

His bald question made her swallow painfully and then stare around the room while she searched for a suitable reply. She didn't find it.

"Why don't you answer me?" He shook her arm, jerking her gaze back to his set features.

"I . . . I don't know what you mean. That's all it was, really. We're not in love with each other or . . . or anything."

The stammered statement ignited a cold blaze in his eyes. "Paula, what's happening between us is not casual. Is it?"

The question was rhetorical. They both knew that what he'd said was true. Only things were going too fast. She couldn't examine her feelings closely or admit out loud what she was beginning to suspect about them. She wouldn't! Setting her jaw like a stubborn child, Paula looked away.

Exasperated, Ben shot her a fierce look. "Answer me, will you?" When she still refused to respond, his angular countenance darkened ominously. "Then I'll make you answer."

He hauled her to him and his head swooped so that his mouth could cover hers. Paula tried to pull back, but it was no use. Ben was far stronger than she and determined to have his way. This was not friendly persuasion; it was a lover's command. After only a moment her struggles became weak, nothing but a mere pretense that they both knew was just for show.

Hotly his kiss deepened, and Paula's lips parted beneath its probing assault. She could hear the thud of his heart. Or was it hers? She wasn't sure. She only knew that her body was trembling with emotions so tangled that she couldn't begin to unravel them. But above the welter, one feeling quickly surfaced and held sway. A piercing excitement quickened deep within her. Tiny flames licked downward. With a hoarse groan, she put her arms around his neck and kissed him back.

Ben's mouth became even more demanding. Like a man dying of thirst who'd stumbled upon a lush oasis, he was drinking from her. As the draining, overpowering kiss went on, his hands shaped her body to his. Restlessly they traveled from her back to her sides, where her breasts were crushed against his chest. Then his sinewy hands moved to her buttocks. At first they stayed outside the terry-cloth material of her shift, content with merely pressing her loins to his. It wasn't long, though, before he lost patience with that and pulled the material up so that his strong fingers could knead and mold the yielding flesh of her soft bottom.

There was no way Paula could deny her response. The flames were no longer tiny. Hot bursts of excitement flared along her nerve paths. Through her shift, she could feel every inch of Ben. Still flattened against his broad, naked chest, her breasts throbbed and her nipples hardened. His hips, which had begun to slowly grind against hers, awakened a dark, answering rhythm in her blood and made her pulse jerk into a frenzied dance. Then he'd pulled the fabric of her shift up past her waist so that she could feel the stiff denim of the frayed cutoffs he wore. Against her bare stomach their coarse texture was startlingly erotic, and she was blazingly aware of the imperative rigidity of his manhood beneath them.

Paula's legs went weak, her weight sagged, and before she was even fully conscious of what was happening, Ben had lowered her to the floor and positioned himself above her. She looked up at him dazedly, her pupils dilated, her mouth blooming from his passionate kiss.

"Now will you answer me?" he demanded thickly.

Like a sleepwalker who'd just tripped on her own feet, she continued to gaze up at his darkly flushed face in confusion. "What was the question?" she finally managed.

"Last night, was it nothing but a one-night stand?"

"No."

His eyes compelled her. "Did it matter to both of us?"

"Yes."

"Enough so that we're both willing to make a few sacrifices in order to explore the issue?" When her reply didn't come swiftly he nipped at the hollow of her throat, dipping his tongue into the sensitive, beating declivity like a bee determined to search out pollen.

Paula breathed in his masculine scent, a heady compound of musky earth and vital, healthy flesh and long days beneath a burning tropic sun—the fragrance of life itself. Her lids fluttered closed. "Yes," she said on a drawn-out sigh.

He reared his head. "Is that a deal?"

"Yes."

His eyes were on her lips, and once more his mouth began to lower toward hers. "All right, then let's start our explorations right now."

Paula was more than willing. It had taken him all of four minutes to reawaken last night's searing desire. Her loose terry dress was now up somewhere around her rib cage, and she was hardly even conscious of the fact. While Ben's weight pressed her lower body hard against the rug, with a single effortless movement, he raised himself on his elbows and began to slip the crumpled garment off her entirely. As his hands lifted it from her, she was bathed in a swirl of sensations. There was the nubbly, slightly prickly feel of the carpet against her back and bare bottom, and there was the exhilarating pressure of Ben's loins welded to hers and the thrust of the blatant arousal still imprisoned behind his zippered shorts. His thighs, hard as oak and covered with short dark hair, rubbed against her smooth skin. He'd even hooked one of his feet around hers so that their ankles were locked.

Suddenly her straining breasts were freed. There was a rush of cool air followed by moist warmth as Ben's mouth closed around a swollen nipple. Moaning with pleasure as he sucked, Paula lifted her hands and slipped them beneath the waistband of his shorts. He wore no underwear. As she realized this, her fingers splayed and moved restlessly against the smooth marble of his small, hard buttocks.

"Paula, every time I touch you, my blood starts to boil," he whispered urgently. "Right now I'm so over-heated I'm about to explode."

"Yes," she answered, knowing exactly what he meant. Her own temperature had quickly shot to the danger point.

He shifted so that she could reach around and un-snap his shorts, then drew in his breath sharply as her seeking fingers moved within the constricted material. The shaft of his manhood was hard and sheathed in warm satin. As she stroked its pulsing length, she felt him tremble with the same mounting excitement that was almost making her teeth chatter. Feverishly she fumbled to push the cutoffs away. But Ben was sud-denly out of forbearance. Swiftly he rolled to one side and stripped away the garment. Then, naked and magnificent, he returned to her.

Neither of them wanted the leisurely, exploratory lovemaking that had characterized their coming to-gether the night before. Neither had the patience for such restraint. Their needs were too urgent. Her heart beating furiously, Paula opened her thighs and Ben settled himself between them. Then, after one swift, questioning look, he plunged deep within her.

She received him with a shuddering gasp of plea-sure. Her breath hissed between her teeth, and her knees came up to lock tight around his waist. Within the silken prison of her receptive body, he paused only for a moment before starting to drive for his pleasure and hers. The urgency of his fiery, deeply penetrating strokes spared neither of them. There was no com-promise, but Paula wanted none, needed none. Lost in the fierce splendor of their coupling, she closed her eyes tight, clung to his straining back and searched for the fulfillment his relentless strokes promised.

The contract was met. Like some gorgeous creature of the deep rising to leap in a joyful, triumphant pinwheel of glittering spray, what they both sought surfaced and exploded into a billion shining bursts of delight.

"Paula!"

Dimly through the glowing tumult, she heard Ben call her name and knew with profound satisfaction that he was finding something akin to the glory he was giving her.

They clung, breathing the musky scent of each other's body and listening as their pounding hearts began to slow against each other's breast.

Finally the world settled back into place. Paula opened her eyes and focused on the corded muscle of Ben's shoulder. A pale blue vein was just visible, and she reached out a finger to stroke it lightly. She felt him breathe deeply and then he rolled with her so that all at once she found herself sprawled atop him. Hesitantly she raised her head and looked down into his face, wondering what she would see.

Behind a half-closed screen of smoky lashes, his eyes were vividly blue. And they were posing a question.

When she didn't immediately respond to it, he asked the question out loud. "Well?"

Her long hair hung around their heads like a pale gold curtain, giving their confrontation an odd, intense privacy. "What do you want me to say?" Her voice was so husky that it sounded unfamiliar, as though she were somewhere deep down in a well.

"I want you to say that you're not going to run out on me like you tried to do this morning."

She fought to steady her breathing. Her heart was still fluttering in her chest. "Ben, I have Nat to consider. I can't sneak across to your house—not even for this."

"Why do you use the word 'sneak'? Why can't we see each other openly? Go to dinner? Go on dates?"

"Because in no time flat word would get around that I was sleeping with you."

"All right, then we'll just have to think of something else."

"Like what?"

"Give me some time." His gaze hadn't wavered yet. "I'll work it out and call you tonight. We'll talk about it."

When she looked doubtful, he slowly quirked an eyebrow and then barked a humorless laugh. "For God's sake, do you think that Bernadette Carstairs has your phone tapped?"

"No, of course not. But—"

"But nothing!" Ben's forearm hooked behind her neck, and he crushed her lips to his. She resisted for only an instant. Then, with a sigh, she surrendered to the passion once more starting to bubble up between them.

8

BEN FLIPPED ON THE TURN SIGNAL and then slanted a look at the beautiful but silent blonde in the passenger seat next to him. "We'll be there in a few minutes."

"Oh."

"Yes, 'oh.' Paula, we've been traveling in this car for over an hour. In all that time I've tried just about every conversational gambit in my repertoire. You haven't responded to any with more than a monosyllable or two. Either I'm losing my touch or you're developing lockjaw."

She glanced at him apologetically. "I'm sorry."

"I don't want you to feel sorry. I want you to be happy that we're finally getting to spend a little unsupervised time together. You are glad, aren't you? Or have you changed your mind again?"

"It's not that. It's just . . . Oh, Ben, this whole situation is so new to me. I've never told lies before in order to spend an illicit weekend with the man across the street. I guess I just don't know how to behave." She turned her head and looked out the car window at the flat, sandy Eastern Shore countryside gliding past.

Ben said in a patient tone, "You told Nat and your mother that you were going on a field trip. Well, you weren't lying. That's what you're doing."

Paula had to laugh. "Somehow, 'field trip' is not the term I'd choose for this little adventure."

"Why not?" he inquired tongue in cheek. "We are taking a trip in order to gather some data firsthand."

"I know all about your hands." Paula turned back toward him and playfully slapped at his knee. "They should be declared illegal."

Ben caught her fingers in his and gave them a squeeze. "For what it's worth, your word 'illicit' is not the term to describe what I have planned for this weekend, either."

"Oh? Then what would you call it?

"I call it an opportunity for us to get to know each other a little better, and I'm not referring to sex. We're already quite well aware that lightning flashes between us every time we touch. Of course I want to sleep with you. But if the word 'illicit' has got you tied up in knots, then I'll arrange for separate rooms."

Paula's eyebrows shot up. When Ben had called to propose this weekend on the Eastern Shore and then bullied her into going along with the idea, she'd been sure he'd intended for them to spend most of their time in bed. It had never occurred to her that he might be willing to accept a more platonic arrangement.

"You're kidding!"

"Giving up the chance for a night with you is no joke," he retorted with a pained chuckle. "But if that's what it takes to prove I like you for other reasons than your delectable body, then so be it." He winked. "I really do want to know more about you than your bra size, and I flatter myself that you might feel the same about me."

"I've never been interested in your bra size."

Ben met that sally with perfect aplomb. "Maybe some day you'll loosen up and tell me just exactly what it is about me that does interest you. In the meantime, Oxford is a charming old town and far enough away from Parcel Court, I hope, so you can relax. Tell you what, if you promise to do that, I'll pledge not to lay a single lustful finger on you."

"Maybe I like your lustful fingers." Paula had surprised herself with that remark, but now that it was out, she looked at him sideways through her lashes, and the corners of her mouth twitched. Though she was flattered by this virtuous pledge of Ben's, she wasn't honestly sure she liked it at all.

His blue eyes gleamed. "Then let me put it this way," he replied silkily. "My dear Ms Kirk, you're in charge of our arrangements this weekend. Do you want separate rooms?"

"No. Since we're not exactly strangers, that would be ridiculous as well as expensive, and my Scotch blood rebels at the idea."

"I've always admired thrifty women. Okay then, we'll be roommates. How about beds? Singles or a double?"

Paula slanted him another sideways look. Just how much of this was for real, she wondered. Ben Gallagher was a very virile man. She couldn't believe he'd whisk a widow away for a romantic weekend and be willing to just sightsee and make small talk. A sudden mischievous impulse made her decide it would be amusing to call his bluff.

"Singles, I think."

Now it was Ben's eyebrows that shot up. He'd made this gesture to reassure Paula, but he hadn't expected her to take him up on it. "You're sure about that?"

"You did give me the option. Are you going to tell me that you didn't mean it?"

He hadn't really meant it, but he wasn't going to admit the fact. "I never make empty gestures. All right, roomie, separate beds. But if you should decide that's not the way you want it, all you have to do is whistle." He produced a very convincing leer. "You know how to do that, don't you?"

Paula had no trouble recognizing the reference. "I just put my lips together and blow," she said, quoting Lauren Bacall's famous line from the old Humphrey Bogart movie.

They both laughed and were still teasing each other when Ben turned off Route 50 onto the side road that led to the Chesapeake Bay's historic river country. Here the scene once again changed character. Though the land remained flat, it was no longer barren looking. Tall stands of oak and pine lined the two-lane highway. Occasionally Paula glimpsed a stately looking colonial mansion. As this part of the Chesapeake had been settled since the seventeenth century, she guessed that many of these were old tobacco plantations that overlooked the estuarial rivers that cut deeply into this ragged section of shore.

When she asked, Ben confirmed her hypothesis. "Yes, there's a lot of old money in these parts."

"You sound very knowledgeable. Have you spent much time in the area?"

"I grew up around here."

Paula turned and stared. "I had no idea. Is that why you wanted to come back—to relive old times?"

"Hardly." Ben's expression was rueful. "My family didn't have any of that old money I mentioned. My father made his living with an oyster boat. It's a hard life. Believe me, when I won a scholarship that took me away from shucking oysters, I was one very relieved young man."

Paula's eyes widened. This information cast a whole new light on Ben. "Does your family still live in these parts?"

"No. My father was the last of the Gallaghers, and he died a few years back. My ex-wife's folks have settled somewhere around Cambridge, but I haven't kept in touch with them. Katy paid them a visit last weekend." Ben cast her a pointed look. "I haven't been back here in many years, but I didn't bring you to revisit my past. I just thought it would be a nice place for us to be together."

When they finally reached the outskirts of Oxford, Paula found herself agreeing. The little old town, with its brick sidewalks, preserved colonial and Federal houses, neat herb gardens and boxwood hedges, was straight out of a bygone era. Since Oxford was surrounded by water on three sides, its quiet, old-fashioned thoroughfares were ringed by picturesque marinas.

The Robert Morris Inn, where Ben had made reservations, was situated at the foot of the town and looked out on the Avon River.

"Oh, it's charming!" Paula exclaimed when Ben's car pulled to a stop in front of the rectangular, curry-colored building. She'd heard about the inn, of course.

Built in 1710, it was famous for its colonial charm. The exterior lived up to its reputation, she thought as she gazed around at the white second-floor balcony and dormer windows.

Inside, the place was even more appealing. While Ben registered, Paula walked around admiring the antique furniture, the white-washed walls and the woodwork, which had been painted a blue-gray. She ran a hand down the gleaming banister of the staircase, which she'd been told was original to the building. Then she peeked into the dining room. With its burgundy painted woodwork, elegant old-fashioned wallpaper and widely spaced tables covered with tablecloths, it was an appealing setting for a meal.

That night, after a delicious candlelit dinner at the inn, Paula and Ben strolled down to the waterfront. They sat talking and watching the water wash gently against a thin strip of beach. "What is it about water?" Paula murmured. "I could sit here forever looking at the moonlight reflecting off it."

"I know what you mean," Ben agreed. "I've seen rivers all over the world. It doesn't seem to matter where they are. At night they're all beautiful and mysterious. This one, though, seems very special," he added, rubbing his cheek lightly against the top of her silky head. "That's because you're here with me."

Paula leaned back against him, enjoying the shelter of his arms and the clean, masculine scent that clung to him.

"The suite you got for us is beautiful," she said a little later as they headed back toward the hotel. "But we don't really need so much room, and two double beds seems awfully extravagant," she added impishly.

Ben's arm was draped around her shoulders. "Somehow I couldn't bring myself to ask for singles. I decided to leave our options open."

"I see." Paula suppressed a giggle. She had no intention of allowing Ben to sleep alone tonight, and doubtless he knew it. But it was fun to play this game with him. It made her feel young and lighthearted, which was the effect he had on her generally.

Their suite really was lovely. Furnished with antiques, it had a small sitting room, a spacious bedroom and a big old-fashioned bath.

"I'm sleepy," Paula declared after they'd climbed the wide, pine-planked stairs to the second floor and shut their door behind them. She strolled into the bedroom and headed for the four-poster on the right, where she'd laid her suitcase. Earlier, she'd hung up the two dresses she'd brought, but she hadn't yet bothered to unpack her night things.

Ben eyed the bed on the left, where his suitcase reposed. "If you're really going to make me sleep in that thing by myself, I'll have to press a hundred push-ups before I can even hope to get my eyes to close."

"You can do that many push-ups?" Paula gave him an interested look.

"In moments of extreme sexual frustration," he explained as he took off his jacket and loosened his tie, "I become Superman."

"You're the one who suggested we sleep apart," Paula managed to point out with a straight face. "You wanted to prove that you weren't just interested in my body."

He was standing across the room, watching her closely. "I didn't suggest we sleep apart, I merely gave you the option. And it's true that I'm not just interested in your body. I want all of you," he added, his gleaming gaze taking a hungry tour of her and lingering on the thrust of her breasts beneath the soft jersey top she wore. "*Including* your gorgeous body!"

Paula turned away and pretended to search through her suitcase. She was tingling all over from the caress of Ben's eyes, and she knew that her cheeks were flushed. "I think I'll change into my night things," she said. "Do you mind if I take the bathroom first?"

"Be my guest."

Lifting some gauzy material from her bag, she walked across the room without looking back at him. When she was safely behind the closed bathroom door, she leaned against it a moment. Then she shook out the garment she'd brought with her and held it out at arm's length.

After she'd agreed to take this trip with Ben, she'd gone shopping. The nightgowns she normally wore were chaste affairs made of white cotton or printed flannel. But the outfit she held in her hands was black silk, lavished with lace. Styled low in the back and crisscrossed with spaghetti straps, it had a provocative front slit. The nightgown had cost a fortune, but it had been worth it, Paula decided as she stood in front of the mirror a few minutes later.

Slowly she ran a brush through her hair and then draped her long blond tresses around her shoulders. They made a striking contrast with the slinky black gown. Through the lace that softened the bodice, her breasts were clearly visible, and every time she moved, the slit in front parted to reveal tantalizing glimpses of creamy thigh. Paula hardly recognized the woman reflected in the glass. This was no post-thirty, boring housewife looking back at her, but a golden-haired temptress.

When she returned to the bedroom, Ben's reaction was gratifying. Stripped to the waist and wearing only pajama bottoms, he was actually doing push-ups. But when he caught sight of her, he froze. His sinewy arms straight, his body tautly parallel to the floor, he turned his head and for a long moment simply stared. Then, emitting a low whistle between his teeth, he got to his feet and stalked toward her.

"If you really wanted me to stay out of your bed, you shouldn't have worn that thing," he warned in a husky voice. Stepping close, he spanned her narrow waist with his hands and stood gazing down at her.

Impulsively Paula reached up and wound her arms around his neck. "Ben, I've put my lips together."

His whole body stiffened. "What?"

"Can't you hear me?" She directed a stream of warm breath against his ear, stirring the silvery tendrils that waved around it. "I'm whistling."

There was a breathless pause. "You'll never make the Boston Symphony," he growled. "But it certainly is music to my ears." He let his hands drift down to the sleek swell of her hips and then hauled her even closer. "Are you sure?"

"Of course I'm sure. You never doubted that you'd be spending the night in my bed, did you?"

"I didn't think you would be so cruel as to keep me away, but at the same time, I really did want to prove that being with you is as important to me as what happens between us physically. You believe that, don't you?"

She was surprised by the earnest tone of his voice, and her arms tightened around his neck. "Stop talking and kiss me, you fool," she whispered.

As his lips melded with hers, he scooped her up and carried her to the bed. "All right," he said thickly, "tomorrow I'll be your friend and companion. But tonight, Paula, tonight I'm going to be your lover. And it's going to be a night to remember."

THEIR HOURS TOGETHER in the sweet darkness of their bedroom were exactly what he'd promised, and so was the following day. Oxford, which had been built as a port of entry in 1694, was a delightful town to explore. In the morning Paula and Ben wandered about visiting the museum and the boatyards. In the afternoon they took their car across the river on the Tred Avon ferry, the oldest free-running ferry in the United States. When they reached the other side, they drove to St. Michaels, a quaint but bustling port that featured boutiques and traditional architecture along with a number of seafood restaurants overlooking its small jewel of a harbor.

Through it all, Ben was a wonderful companion, charming, easy to be with and a pleasure to behold in white pants and a faded blue chambray shirt. Obviously sincere about getting to know Paula better, he made every effort to draw her out. Over lunch he even laughingly taught her how to eat crabs.

"Didn't you tell me that you moved here from Pennsylvania with your husband ten years ago?" Ben shook his head. "I can't believe you've lived in this state for that long and haven't yet learned to enjoy an epicurean treat that's one of the great traditions in Maryland eating."

Doubtfully Paula eyed the crustacean he'd ordered for her lunch. With its round body and dangling legs, it resembled an oversize pink spider.

"You have to admit, it's not very appealing to look at. And with all that shell . . ."

Ben's sapphire eyes smiled into hers. "Surely you've learned by now that the pleasures hardest to come by are the ones most worth having."

Paula wondered what he meant by that. It couldn't refer to the pleasures of the previous night. Ben was such a consummate lover that he'd made those easy to achieve. She pointed at the crab and said, "I thought you told me making a meal of that thing was going to be easy."

"It is. Like everything else in life, it's all in knowing how to go about it. Here, I'll show you." And with that he quickly taught her the five steps to dismantling and eating a steamed crab. Though Paula remained dubious, when he got to the last stage, which revealed large, succulent chunks of meat, she had to admit it was worth the effort.

While Paula sipped at her wine, Ben ordered a second glass of beer. As they washed their crabs down and looked out at the sailboats coming in and out of the harbor, they talked of many things—their childhoods, their memories of high school and college, their tastes in books and movies. They even spent half an hour arguing their quite different opinions on the international situation.

However, two subjects seemed to be off limits. The mention of headlines made Paula remember the notes on *Ejercito de los Puños* that she'd stumbled on. But when she tried to draw Ben out about his experiences in South America and his interest in the politics of the area, he politely made it clear that was not a subject he wished to discuss. Even though she suspected he was still involved in some mysterious fashion, there was no way she could find out for certain. And that reminded her of how little she really knew about this man who'd become her lover.

Likewise, when Ben asked a few leading questions about the long illness Paula's husband had suffered, she clammed up tight.

"What was your married life like before he got sick?" Ben queried.

They were on their way back to Oxford, standing on the upper deck of the ferry and watching the white froth churned by the boat's wake. Below them some children leaned over the rail and threw potato chips to seabirds that were following the vessel and screaming eerie entreaties.

"My life with Tim was very busy," Paula finally answered. "Because of his job, he was always being invited to things, so we attended a lot of social functions together."

"My guess is that would be hard on you. You don't seem the social type."

"No," she admitted, her eyes on the hazy outline of the distant shore they were leaving behind. "Tim was a very warm, outgoing person, and I'm somewhat reserved. But that's one of the reasons we were happy together. We complemented each other."

There were many more questions Ben wanted to ask. He wanted to understand better what she'd gone through during her husband's illness, but some sixth sense warned him to hold his tongue. Watching a loved one slowly die must have been an agonizing experience, he told himself. But just how agonizing? Was that piece of her past affecting her present in some way he didn't yet quite comprehend?

Because of Nat, Ben could understand her reluctance to compromise her reputation on Parcel Court. But he had a hunch there was more to it than that. Sometimes she seemed as skittish about their affair as a child who wanted to toast marshmallows but was afraid to because she'd once been burnt. He was delighted that last night and today she'd seemed to cast off her worries and inhibitions.

She was so lovely, he thought as they left the ferry and headed back to the hotel. In pink pedal pushers and a loose checked shirt tied at the waist, she looked about eighteen. But he was well aware that she was fully a woman.

Gently he tugged on her pale gold braid. "It's getting late. Want to change for dinner?"

"Yes." She nodded and linked her arm with his as they crossed the strand. "Ben, this has been a wonderful day."

"I thought so, too. Now let's make it a wonderful evening. And after that, another wonderful night."

She shot him a quick, startled look. Then, as her cheeks went pink, she laughed and leaned against his seductive warmth. "All right," she agreed, "let's do that!"

IT WAS STRANGE, Paula thought later. After the first time she'd made love with Ben at his house, she'd worried about becoming a Ben Gallagher junkie. But it was the weekend in Oxford that made her an addict. Before their getaway, an aura of mystery had clung to him. That in combination with his aggressive sexuality had made her a bit nervous of him.

In Oxford she'd gotten to know him as a man who could be both tender and vulnerable and who had a painfully strong sense of his own shortcomings. He made no pretense that the failure of his first marriage was anything but his doing, and that paradoxically disarmed her.

On one occasion, Paula had asked, "Katy looks like her mother, doesn't she?"

"Yes. Judy was a sweet little redhead, too. Only Katy has my eyes. Judy's were the color of dark sherry."

Paula waited for the stabbing jealousy that twisted through her to settle down. "You must have loved your wife. Do you still think about her?"

Ben had answered her first question with unnerving honesty. "I adored Judy. But the timing was wrong for us. Katy was on the way when we married. I was hungry for life and too young to settle down. What Judy needed and had every right to expect, I couldn't give." He stared off into the distance. "I've occasionally thought that if we met now, things would be different. But it's too late for that. Judy's made a new life for herself. She's happy with it, and God knows she deserves it, so I'm glad."

Paula studied his profile. He hadn't answered her second question, so she cleared her throat and asked it again. "Do you still think about her?"

He looked at her sharply. "Why do you ask? Are you going to make my day and tell me that you're jealous?"

"I'm just curious."

He didn't hedge. "I've learned not to dwell on the past. I'm well aware that I made a lot of mistakes, but except perhaps for Katy, there's nothing I can do about them. I've closed the book on those years. Paula, it's the future I'm looking to now."

Not knowing how to respond, she quickly changed the subject, but she wondered what sort of future Ben had in mind. Surely it didn't include her or Parcel Court. Since coming back from Oxford, he'd disappeared twice more in as many weeks, vanishing for two or three days, giving no explanation of his whereabouts and refusing to discuss the reasons for his absence. It was obvious that he led some sort of secret life, so she was convinced he couldn't be serious about running a suburban pet shop. No, this was just an episode, an experiment of which he'd soon tire.

But it didn't matter that their affair had no future, she told herself—nor that there were things about Ben's world that he wouldn't share. Paula felt as if her whole life had been bound up with obligation and responsibility. Her times with Ben made her feel young and deliciously wicked and most of all—unfettered. With him she could live for the sweetness of the moment and not think beyond it.

And what honeyed moments there were! Paula loved being with him. When she wasn't with him, he was in her thoughts. So overwhelming was her fascination for him that several times over the next couple of weeks she found herself doing precisely what had originally most horrified her. After night fell and Nat was safely tucked away in bed, she would slip across the street to spend an hour or two with Ben.

They didn't always make love on these occasions. As often as not they would just sit together on his patio, drinking a glass of wine and talking quietly. Once he spent what seemed like forever brushing her hair, murmuring sweet words and kissing her throat and neck and ears between each long, sensuous stroke. Each stolen moment was precious—all the more so for being fleeting and, yes, "illicit."

The rational part of her knew that she was living in a dream world. She was a practical person who led an ordinary life. She hadn't been made to indulge in forbidden summer idylls. It was bound to all come crashing down around her ears.

Yet, though she cautioned herself, she repeatedly closed her mind to her own warnings. The lover who beckoned was too compelling to forswear in the name of prudence and propriety. Surely what she and Ben had together could be preserved for a little longer, she would tell herself. Surely she had another few weeks to indulge this delicious fantasy. But it wasn't to be.

One afternoon, quite by chance, Paula ran into Ben in the aisles of the grocery store at Martin Square. She was reaching for a jar of spaghetti sauce when his cart scraped hers. Their eyes met and she started to laugh.

"Watch where you're going with that grocery cart, sir. This is not the Indy Five Hundred."

"It's not my fault that my steering was affected by the sight of a beautiful blonde."

Like a pair of teenagers deep in the toils of first love, they beamed at each other. For them, the rest of the world didn't exist. They never noticed that Bernadette Carstairs, her eyes narrowed, was approaching them from the other end of the aisle. Paula didn't look up and see the woman until she'd whirled past.

Three days later Nat came home with a troubled expression on his face. Paula was making a salad for dinner, absentmindedly shredding lettuce and chopping tomatoes while she thought about the plans she and Ben had begun to make for a weekend in Cape May.

"Mom?"

"Umm. Did you and Johnny have a good time with your bikes this afternoon?"

There was a silence that cut through Paula's preoccupation and made her look up from the green onions she was rinsing.

"We didn't do much riding," Nat finally answered. He was wearing a baseball cap, which was pulled low over his forehead, shadowing his eyes.

"What did you do?"

"We, uh…" He picked up an envelope that was lying on the counter and began to fiddle with it. "We watched some TV in his game room and played cards."

Paula glanced at the clock and then lined up the ends of the onions on the chopping board. "You're home early," she commented as she lifted her knife. "I wasn't expecting you for another half hour."

"Yeah, well something Johnny said made me mad. So I left."

"What was it?" She gave him a sympathetic look, but privately she was thinking that kids quarreled over the most ridiculous things. Probably this was a dispute that would be patched up by tomorrow.

"It was about you . . . about you and Mr. Gallagher."

The knife slipped and a crimson spot of blood welled up over the pad of Paula's thumb. As though it held some secret message that she needed to decode, she stared fixedly at it. "Nat, I thought you and Mr. Gallagher had become such good friends that you called him Ben," she mumbled.

"Yeah, well I haven't seen him so much lately. He hasn't got any good fish in his store."

"He hasn't?"

"Nope. Just the usual stuff."

Paula knew that wasn't true. Ben had stocked a spectacular selection. She rinsed her thumb and then turned toward Nat. "What did Johnny say about me and Mr. Gallagher?"

Nat didn't meet her eyes. Instead, he gazed doggedly down at the corner of the envelope he was clutching. "It was just some dumb stuff he overheard when his mother's bridge group got together last night."

Bernadette belonged to that bridge group. Paula took a deep breath. "Like what?"

"Oh, just some dumb stuff...about how you and Mr. Gallagher were fooling around. I knew it was just a bunch of lies. Besides, you don't even like Mr. Gallagher very much and you still miss Dad." He took off his cap and gave her a direct look. Even though the eye contact was meant as a gesture of confidence, Paula could see the fear and doubt lurking behind it.

"Of course I still miss your father," she said very gently. "But I don't dislike Mr. Gallagher, you know. He's been very nice to you, Nat."

"Oh, sure." He frowned, and now the worried, defensive look in his hazel eyes was unmistakable. "He's okay, but you wouldn't...you wouldn't fool around with him or anything. You're not like that. You're special."

Paula felt something deep within her slowly tear. What could she say to her son that wouldn't be a lie? He'd been through so much. Even though he'd been too young to really understand what was happening, he'd had to watch his father die. The atmosphere of his home during that period had been heavy with unspeakably painful emotions—not a very wholesome environment for a child with few defenses against the ills of the world. But even though he'd had nightmares for a long time afterward and still had them occasionally, Nat had survived. Now he was beginning to seem like a healthy, relatively happy kid again. How could she allow her own selfish desires to threaten that?

Paula pressed her hands together so that the blood that had once more pooled on her thumb smeared across her fingers. "Nat, I love you very much. I would never do anything to hurt or embarrass you. That's a promise."

He looked at her doubtfully for a moment, but then his expression cleared. "Oh, I knew that all along, Mom. Johnny's just full of it."

"Full of what?" Paula managed a smile.

Nat's return grin was impish. "Oh, you know what I mean."

"Yes," she retorted, reaching out to tousle his hair. "I'm afraid I do."

She was afraid she also knew what this meant to her secret romance with Ben Gallagher. It meant that it was over. Now all she had to do was explain her decision to him.

That night she made what she told herself had to be her last midnight trek to the house across the street. Ben was waiting for her on the patio, and when she stepped inside the privacy fence, he swept her into his arms.

"I'm so glad you called," he murmured against her hair. "I've been thinking about you all day." Before she could move away, he lowered his mouth to the gentle slope where her neck and shoulder joined.

Though the night was warm, Paula shivered. "Ben," she said in a husky voice, "I have to talk to you."

"Talk away." He caught the lobe of her ear between his teeth. "I've been wanting to hear your voice. Tell me you'll go with me to Cape May next weekend. There's a wonderful old hotel there with a wraparound veranda. We can sit in rocking chairs and rock and tell each other our life stories."

That was a joke, Paula thought. There were things about his life that Ben was never going to tell her. Steeling herself, she shook her head and then placed her hands on his shoulders so that she could push herself away. "That's not what I've come to say to you."

Catching the strained note in her voice, Ben frowned and scrutinized her face through the shadows. "Would you like a drink? I can fix us gin and tonics. There's fresh lime in the refrigerator."

Once again, she shook her head. This was going to be very hard. Oh, why had she allowed him to overwhelm her that first time? If she'd had the strength to make her refusal stick then, they wouldn't have become so deeply involved and this wouldn't be so painful. But even as she entertained the thought, she was aware that she didn't regret having known this lover. She only regretted having to part from him.

"Ben, listen to me. Something happened today." Quickly, and with almost no inflection, Paula recounted her conversation with Nat. When she finished, he was scowling.

"That woman ought to be called out at dawn. We haven't been necking on the street. You've been careful to the point of paranoia. Where did she get her information?"

"I don't know. It's true we've tried to be discreet, but she has antennae where these things are concerned. She could have seen me come over to your place." Paula made a little gesture of futility. "It doesn't matter how she found out. What matters is that she's putting this story around and it's hurting my son. It has to be stopped."

"How do you propose to do that?" He was studying her with narrowed eyes.

Paula took a deep breath and met his gaze. "If there's nothing to the story that we're having an affair, it will die on its own. I propose to stop it by not seeing you again."

His breath came out in a hiss. "You don't mean that."

"Yes, yes, I do. I should never have let this . . . us . . . happen. It hasn't anywhere to go and it has to end."

Once the words were out, they seemed to hang in the air like a suspended sword. For long, thudding heartbeats, Ben said nothing. As Paula waited in tense anticipation, she was suddenly aware of the night around them. Leaves rustled faintly in the light breeze that had sprung up. An owl hooted and insects called out secret messages. Occasionally the velvety darkness was punctuated by the intimate flash of a lightning bug. Above the trees a ragged froth of cloud drifted across the moon's sadly battered face.

But most of all she was acutely aware of Ben. Though he was not yet giving expression to his anger, she could almost feel it building. Then, like a clenched fist, it reached out to her.

"Because of a ridiculous piece of gossip, you've marched across here to say goodbye? After what we've been to each other, you're willing to cut me loose over something like this?"

To try to stop their trembling, Paula clenched her hands and wrapped her arms tightly around her waist. "I know it all seems ridiculous to you. We're so very different. You're a man with no ties, and you don't have to worry about protecting your reputation. But you have to understand it from my point of view. My first responsibility is to Nat. He's at a very sensitive age. I can't let an affair embarrass and hurt him."

Though the darkness obscured the expression on Ben's face, a sliver of moonlight exposed the angry glitter in his eyes. And something else. Pain? Could her words possibly have hurt a man like Ben Gallagher? She couldn't believe it.

"Is that all you think we're having—an affair? Haven't you left something out?"

"What?"

"There's another word that goes with 'affair.' It's 'love,' Paula. The usual term is 'love affair.'"

Astounded, she took a step backward. "We never pretended to be in love."

"There's been no pretense in anything I've said to you." He paused. "Or done with you. Can you tell me the same?"

She wanted to look away from Ben's eyes, but they held her. "I don't know what you mean," she whispered.

"Did you think this was just an affair that was going nowhere—that had nowhere to go?"

"Yes, yes, that's what I thought. What else was I to think?"

"What else? My God, woman, you don't have a very high opinion of me, do you?" Ben glared at her. Then suddenly his expression changed. He grasped her by the shoulders and gazed down at her earnestly. "You just told me that Nat was at a sensitive age. Well, so am I, Paula. I'm looking at the second half of my life. I don't want to go on being a man with no ties. There's a simple solution to this problem. Marry me. Be my wife."

Her insides were already tied in knots. But Ben's words made them writhe in even more tangled confusion. "You can't be serious!"

"I'm perfectly serious."

"But it's only been a month. We . . ." She was going to say, "We hardly know each other," but then she realized how ridiculous that would sound. In one sense they knew each other very well, but in so many other ways they were still strangers. Mutely she shook her head. "No, Ben, that's impossible."

His grip only tightened. "Why is it impossible? Nat likes me and he needs a father. I think in time he would accept me. And though you pretend otherwise, you need a man, Paula. I think what's happened between us makes that fact clear. We're both lonely people. We both feel an emptiness in our life. Let's fill that gap with each other."

Paula's mind was in a whirl. Surely he couldn't mean what he was saying? Marriage wasn't something to be entered into on a whim as a matter of convenience. To mask her confusion, she reacted to his last statement. "I do not *need* a man," she gritted. "Until you came here, I was getting along fine."

"You call the life you're leading 'getting along fine'?"

"What's wrong with it?" She put her hands on her hips, daring him to answer.

"All right, I'll tell you. You're a mature, beautiful woman and you're wasting your life."

"Oh, that's not true!" Paula was insulted. She was proud of the way she'd picked herself up after Tim's death. Maybe she hadn't put all the pieces together yet, but she was on the way. "I lead a very full life. I have a family and a career, and both are very important to me."

Ben ignored her denial. "I know you love your son, but he's no real company for you. You're rattling around in a big, empty house filled with unpleasant memories and refusing to rejoin the living."

That was too much. "What you're really talking about is sex. Well, for your information, I can be alive without bedding the man across the street."

"Maybe so, but you wouldn't be visiting him if there weren't something about him you liked."

Ignoring that, she doggedly finished her retort. "As for the house, I'd sell it, but it's the only real home Nat has known and with all he's been through, I don't want to uproot him."

"But that's not the real reason," Ben insisted. "You're just using that for an excuse to run away from reality. You're afraid to turn your back on the past and start a new life. You'd rather wall yourself away and cower in fear over what someone like Bernadette Carstairs might say about you."

Paula was so upset by the unfairness of this that she almost stuttered. "You're a fine one to talk about running away from reality. What in the world is a man like you doing with a pet shop? It's ridiculous! You can't possibly imagine that you're going to make a living off it."

"What has my income from the pet shop got to do with this?" His eyes narrowed to dangerous slits. "Is that why you're refusing me? You think I'm all right to have an affair with but not all right to marry because I couldn't provide for you and your son? Is that it?"

In silent outrage, Paula stared at him. Such a thought had never crossed her mind. How could it when the idea of marriage to Ben Gallagher had never even occurred to her? With his mysterious past and his even more mysterious present, he wasn't the kind of man to whom a sensible woman made a commitment. Besides, she had no interest in remarrying—not Ben Gallagher, not anyone. Without another word, Paula turned on her heel and left. Ben didn't try to stop her. He only stood with his feet apart and arms akimbo, seething with frustration.

9

"I THINK IT'S TIME you told me what's wrong," Lynn said, ignoring the menu the waitress had just given her.

Across the table, Paula's expression was guarded. She and her mother often had lunch at the restaurant near Lynn's apartment building. It was a comfortably informal place that featured half-timbered walls, cushiony Leatherette booths and a large selection of nourishing sandwiches and soups.

Paula settled back against her padded bench and looked out the window into the parking lot. "I don't know what you mean."

"This is your mother talking." Lynn reached over and patted an errant strand of her daughter's fair hair back into place. "I've been acquainted with you since before you were in diapers, remember? There's something going on between you and Ben Gallagher."

"How did you..." Paula blurted, and then almost bit her tongue off.

"How did I know?" Looking amused, Lynn gently touched a hand to her own neat gray coif. "My dear, I may be past menopause, but I'm not dead. At that shopping center party of his, the atmosphere between you two was thicker than cream of mushroom soup. He was attracted. And you would have to be blind not to return the favor. Mr. Benjamin Gallagher is a gorgeous hunk of man."

Paula buried her nose in the menu. "I think I'll have the clam chowder and half an egg salad sandwich. How does that sound?"

"Terribly fattening. There's something else. Nat told me about that gossip Bernadette Carstairs is passing out."

Paula's head jerked up. "He did?"

"Yes, he did. Now, will you please stop being so ridiculous and let your mother know what's going on?"

Paula did not immediately comply. While she ordered and then nibbled her way through her lunch, she adroitly parried her mother's penetrating questions. It wasn't until the coffee was served that she finally told her some of what she wanted to know.

"All right, I have been spending some time with Ben Gallagher, but that's all over. I don't intend to see him again."

Her mother's large brown eyes went round. "Why not?"

"Why not?" Unconsciously Paula began toying with her spoon. "It must be obvious why not. Nat's told you about the gossip. I can't have that sort of thing going around to bother him."

"Oh, pooh! Do you mean to tell me that you broke off with a man like Ben Gallagher because of a little gossip?"

Paula passed a hand over her forehead. "Yes. I told him I couldn't see him anymore."

"And what did he have to say?"

Without answering, Paula once again turned and looked out the window. Lynn eyed her daughter shrewdly. "Did that man ask you to marry him?"

I might as well have a transparent head, Paula thought. Even though she was a thirty-one-year-old adult, nothing had changed. She'd never been able to keep a secret from her mother. "Yes, if you must know."

"What was your answer?"

"I refused."

"Why? If you've been seeing him, you must like him."

Paula shot her mother a look of exasperation. "For God's sake, marriage is a serious step. I hardly know the man." Which wasn't quite accurate, but she had no intention of detailing the exact nature of their relationship.

"I don't know how well you know him." Lynn's thin eyebrows lifted ever so slightly. "I didn't get the impression, though, that Gallagher was the sort of man who would propose marriage to a woman with whom he was not well acquainted. I only saw him once, but in my opinion you're crazy to let him get away. A woman needs a husband, and you're not getting any younger, you know. I'd like you to tell me why you're being so foolish."

Maybe Ben and her mother should go into partnership, Paula thought. They were spouting all the same lines. "A woman does not *need* a husband, and I'd like to know why you're grilling me like this."

"Because I care about you, that's why." Leaning forward, Lynn covered Paula's cold hand with one of her warm ones. "You've had me worried for a long time now. Honey, I saw what you went through while Tim was dying. I was proud of the way you stayed strong for him, but I know it left scars. You're a beautiful woman and men are naturally attracted to you. But you've been holding yourself so aloof, putting everything you've got into that job, and I can't help but wonder...." Lynn's voice trailed off, but her far too perceptive gaze was trained on her daughter's pale, tense features.

Paula's mouth trembled and suddenly she felt torn between tears and hysterical laughter. She certainly hadn't been holding herself aloof from Ben. Until that painful night last week when they'd parted in anger, she'd been about as aloof as a cocker spaniel puppy hungry for affection. The last few days had been among the most miserable of her life—which was saying something. It was agonizing to see Ben puttering in his yard and to drive past his house in the evening and know that she might have been having dinner with him on his patio. It was worse to lie alone in bed, reliving the hurtful things they'd said to each other and longing for his touch. But their relationship had been doomed from the start. What must be, must be. For Nat's sake and for her own, she had to be strong.

Gently but firmly removing her hand from Lynn's grasp, Paula laced her fingers together and sat up very straight. "Mother, there are things about Ben Gallagher that make him very unsuitable husband material. He's a mystery man with a history of instability where commitments to women are concerned. But even if that weren't the case, I'm not sure I'm ready to remarry."

Lynn was startled. "Why ever not? Until he got sick, you and Tim were happy together."

"Yes."

"I know those last two years were a nightmare for you."

"They were much worse for Tim." Paula swallowed. "But yes, they were awful. Watching him slip away from me and not being able to do a thing to stop it . . . I'm just putting my life back together now. It's only lately that I've begun to feel whole again." She shook her head. "Mother, I'm not so young and resilient anymore. I couldn't bear to love someone and be so helpless again."

Lynn's expression was sympathetic. "We all lose our loved ones eventually. It's part of living."

"Yes, but Tim was still young. He wasn't ready to die, and it still hurts." Paula's eyes suddenly glistened with tears. "When I first got married, I didn't really understand the meaning of those phrases—'To have and to hold, for better or for worse.' Now I do. Marriage is a lot more than physical attraction, a lot more than just a convenient arrangement. I'm not ready to accept that kind of responsibility again. Right now, I haven't the strength."

"But sweetheart, you're responsible for Nat."

"Yes, and I can handle that. But more, I can't do." Cold and trembling, Paula shook her head, and one burning tear slipped from the corner of her eye.

In growing distress, Lynn stared at her daughter. "What you're really saying is that you don't want to love anybody again. But you can't turn off that part of you. It's like saying no to life."

The statement was so much an echo of something Ben had said that Paula responded as if a nerve had been struck. "It's easy for you to sit there and tell me that, but you never remarried after Daddy died."

"Only because I never came across anyone who made me feel the way he did. Oh, honey, you'll get over this. You'll change your mind when you meet the right man."

But Paula didn't think so. Because, though she had no intention of admitting the fact to her mother, she was beginning to suspect that she'd already met the right man—and lost him.

ANOTHER WEEK DRAGGED PAST. Somehow Paula limped through it. There were, as always, a million things to be done. Nat needed new school clothes. Her own fall things had to be hauled out of the basement and aired. The last days of August were as hot as ever, but seasons in Maryland had a way of changing dramatically. It was entirely possible that a week or two into September the weather would abruptly turn cool.

The Labor Day picnic on Parcel Court was a traditional event marking the change from summer to autumn. Though Nat was looking forward to the annual celebration, Paula was dreading it. Of course, she told herself, there was a good chance that Ben wouldn't attend. But with the determined way he seemed to be trying to make himself a part of the community, it was equally possible that he would.

Bernadette Carstairs had taken on the job of organizing food. When she called Paula to ask whether she wanted to bring a dessert or a salad, Paula opted for a German chocolate cake. It was one of the few things she made that always came out right.

"As far as the meat goes, just bring hot dogs or hamburgers, whatever you and your son enjoy eating," Bernadette instructed her airily. "You needn't worry about a grill. We already have enough—especially since Mr. Gallagher is providing two hibachis."

Paula's heart sank. So he would be there. "Oh," she said stiffly. "That's nice."

There was a coy pause on the other end of the line. "Didn't he mention his hibachis to you?"

"Why no," Paula responded cautiously. "I don't believe I've spoken to Mr. Gallagher in weeks."

It was true enough. Since that night on his patio, she and Ben hadn't exchanged a word, and that had been two weeks ago.

THE DAY OF THE PICNIC was fair and dry with just a hint of fall in the air. Other signs presaged the change of seasons. Isolated leaves on the dogwoods had begun to blush a furious red, and here and there sprays of yellow showed among the green headdresses of the beeches that lined the street. Almost all the summer flowers were gone. Only orange and gold chrysanthemums flamed against the sides of houses.

That afternoon, while Nat licked the bowl, Paula spread the last of the frosting on the cake she'd agreed to make.

"This is yummy," Nat enthused. "You should bake more often."

Paula reached across the counter and wiped a blob of chocolate off his cheek. "I don't have the time or the talent and cake is fattening."

"Johnny's mom bakes cakes and pies and stuff almost every day. She's bringing a bunch of cupcakes to the picnic."

"Johnny's mom weighs two hundred pounds and doesn't have a job."

Above the spoon he was just taking out of his mouth, Nat's freckles seemed to glow. "Yeah," he conceded, "you're a lot prettier than she is, even if you don't bake. And anyway, there's gonna be a lot of good food to eat today. I know because I already checked on what everybody is bringing."

"Trust you," Paula remarked dryly. But she was smiling.

Nat didn't hear. He'd stepped out the side door to peer at the grassy circle at the bottom of the cul-de-sac where the picnic would be held. He came back with sparkling eyes.

"They're already setting stuff up down there and getting the grills going."

"You don't say." Paula wanted to ask if Ben was among them, but she was reluctant to mention his name. Nat, however, had no such inhibitions. He'd been upset enough about the rumors he'd heard to stay away from his new friend for a week. But when a tank of blacklace veiltail angelfish had gone on display at the pet shop, he'd been lured back. For the past few days he'd been referring to Ben by his first name again, the distressing gossip apparently forgotten.

So the whole thing really had been a tempest in a teapot, Paula thought as she carefully placed plastic wrap over the top of the cake. At least, that's what it had been for Nat. "Major cataclysm" would be a better way of describing the turmoil of her emotions.

"I'd better go out there and help Ben," Nat volunteered. "He's got his friend with him, but she doesn't look like she knows how to get charcoal going."

"Oh?" Paula stiffened. "What friend is this?"

"Just some lady he brought," Nat called over his shoulder, and then disappeared through the door.

Dropping verbal grenades was getting to be a habit with her son, Paula reflected as she stood very still in front of her kitchen counter. So Ben was bringing another woman to the neighborhood picnic. Well, why should that be a surprise? He was a very attractive man and not the type to languish long without female companionship. She'd known that.

With quiet steps, Paula walked out of the kitchen and approached the large mirror that hung on the grass-cloth-covered wall in the family room. She had chosen to wear a sleeveless dark blue jersey dress with a scooped neck and a dropped waistline. Though it fitted snug to her breasts, waist and hips, the skirt swirled in lose pleats to the middle of her calves. In the simple but graceful costume her tall willowy body looked like a dancer's. The effect was emphasized by her hair, which on a whim she had coiled in two flat blond braids against her ears.

I look like a Dutch hippie, she thought with a faint smile. Though her appearance wasn't particularly suburban, it pleased her. She was going to have to face Ben in public some time—it might as well be now. Squaring her shoulders, she walked back to the kitchen, picked up the cake and, balancing it in her two hands, headed for the side door.

Nat was right. Ben's lady friend didn't look as if she'd be good at starting charcoal, at least not in that spotless designer silk blouse and those crisp white shorts. But she certainly looked as if she was very competent in a lot of other ways. If Paula had half expected to find a Spanish seductress hanging on Ben's arm, she was disappointed. Yet somehow the neat, attractive brunette who was giving him laughing instructions while he kneeled on the grass to stoke his hibachis seemed even more alarming.

"You're pouring on too much starter," the unknown woman chided in a playful contralto. "There's going to be a big explosion when you throw a match at that."

"Big explosions are part of my ineffable charm," Ben retorted, reaching into his back pocket.

"Just so long as you don't blow your ineffable charm away when you light that bomb!"

Paula wondered who the brunette with the easy repartee was. Obviously she and Ben were on very good terms and had known each other for a while. Apparently Ben hadn't noticed Paula's approach. He hadn't, at any rate, bothered to look in her direction. She turned away from the sound of the twosome's comfortable banter and made a concerted effort to think of other things.

Nat had been right about the food, too, she observed as she moved toward the table in the center of the grassy circle. It was so loaded with delicious-looking dishes that she was going to have trouble finding a spot for the cake. As she made a business of rearranging a fruit salad and a Crockpot full of baked beans, she wondered how she was going to get through the next couple of hours. It was bad enough to have to face Ben again and pretend that there was nothing between them. But to have to do that while he was in the company of another, extremely attractive woman?

Paula looked down at her hands and saw that they were trembling. Quickly she set the cake next to a spinach salad. Then she almost jumped as suddenly the rich timbre of Ben's good-humored voice penetrated her misery. She turned and saw that, hands cupped around his mouth, he was making a general announcement.

"These grills were made for cooking and in ten minutes will be ready to take all comers. So get ready to bring on the hot dogs and hamburgers, folks!"

It certainly didn't sound as if *he* were finding the situation difficult. In fact, from his jovial tone, no one would guess there was a "situation." Once again, Paula stiffened her spine and squared her shoulders. That was the point of this whole exercise, wasn't it? She'd given up her love affair with the man in order to quash any rumors that might hurt Nat. Well, if she could get through the rest of this afternoon with a smiling face, she would have accomplished her goal.

For the next hour Paula was steeled to look as if she were enjoying herself. After the meat was grilled, filling the air with its special aroma redolent of memories of a hundred other summer backyard feasts, everyone loaded paper plates with potato and macaroni salads, tossed greens and deviled eggs.

The children, many of them nephews or nieces or even grandchildren of some of the older couples on the street, clustered together at their own table. The air was filled with the sound of their giggling as they washed down hot dogs and potato chips with gallons of soda pop. Paula waited until Ben and his lady friend were seated before selecting a picnic table as far away as possible so that she wouldn't be forced to listen to their conversation. To her surprise, she was joined almost immediately by Katy. The girl had arrived a few minutes earlier with a nice-looking young man in tow.

"That's Bob," she supplied, setting her plate down next to Paula and hooking a leg over the bench. "He's studying to be a spy."

"Oh?" Paula turned her head.

Bob, who was following a few paces behind, balancing a paper plate piled high with food, shot the little redhead a disgusted look.

"Katy, for God's sake!"

"I know, I know." Katy managed to look charmingly unrepentant. "It's just that I'm an uncomplicated Midwestern type. I can't get used to all this Washington hush-hush stuff." She forked up a bite of potato salad and then turned again to Paula. "Actually, spying was more my father's thing. Bob is just interning at the National Protection Agency in a language program," she confided, naming a very powerful, top secret government organization. "Liz over there is his boss." She glanced in the direction of Ben's brunette companion and then cocked an inquiring eyebrow at Bob who looked distinctly flustered. "Isn't she?"

"Katy, you know I'm not supposed to discuss this." His thick brown eyebrows had snapped together above his green eyes.

"It's okay," the irrepressible redhead cheerfully assured him. "Paula isn't a Russian spy. Are you, Paula?"

Paula had to laugh. "Not that I know about. But your friend is absolutely right. You shouldn't be telling this sort of thing to me."

Now that Katy had, however, Paula couldn't restrain her curiosity. She found her gaze straying back to the table where Ben and his friend were chuckling at each other merrily. So the woman's name was Liz and she worked at the National Protection Agency. That meant she must be very bright as well as very attractive. Paula felt something twist in her stomach. Without realizing it, she snapped a potato chip into a dozen pieces.

"Your father and Bob's boss seem to enjoy each other's company," she murmured. It was despicable to fish like this, but she couldn't seem to help herself.

Katy took the bait. "Oh, Liz and Dad have been pals forever. Before Dad quit active duty and started just consulting, they used to work together all the time. She even went on some missions with him."

"How romantic," Paula mumbled.

But her remark was interrupted by an interjection from an exasperated Bob. "Katy, if you don't close your mouth right now, I'm going to muzzle you!"

Ben's impish daughter made a face calculated to melt all opposition. "Oh, all right! I'll be good. Let's talk about something else." She glanced at another table across the way. "Who is that woman over there with the face like an Airedale and the strange-looking hair?"

Choking back a giggle, Paula followed the direction of her gaze. "That's Bernadette Carstairs."

"Oh, so she's the one!" Katy's eyes sparkled. "I've heard about her. Do you know, Dad told me that when he first moved in here he had his garage full of boxes. Since there was temporarily no room for his car, he had to leave it parked in front of the house for a couple of days. She called him up and told him to move it."

"Some way to welcome a new neighbor," Bob commented.

Paula nodded. "That's par for the course. My husband and I were greeted in similar fashion when we first moved in."

"What a strange woman," Katy mused. "I wonder why she behaves like that. Is she married?"

"No, divorced. She's lived all alone in that big house ever since I've been here."

"Displacement," Bob explained sagely. "She's dissatisfied with her life, so she's taking her frustration out on others."

Katy aimed a flirtatious wink at him. "Oh, is that something I'll learn about in Psychology 101?"

"Well, I certainly hope you'll learn a thing or two, but I have my doubts," Bob retorted, reaching across the table to tweak a fiery curl.

That little exchange led to an animated discussion of the courses Katy planned to take in the fall. It was followed by a colorful report of her impressions of life in the nation's capital. As Paula listened she found herself smiling at the young woman's verve and enthusiasm. It was a blessing to have Katy to talk with and Paula was grateful. She was of course intensely aware of the table where Ben and Liz seemed to be having such a good time together, but Katy's lively company made this part of the afternoon far less painful than Paula had anticipated.

When the main course had been devoured, people drifted back to the food table to select a dessert. Paula had no intention of eating sweets. She had no appetite and had picked at the salads on her plate merely to be polite. Out of the corner of her eye she saw Ben approach the buffet table. Quickly she looked away. There was a hum of appreciative comments as the picnickers made their choices. To Paula's consternation, the low hum was pierced by Nat's shrill, excited voice.

"The German chocolate cake is my Mom's, Ben. Take that. It's the best!"

Paula inhaled sharply and then willed herself not to show her discomfort. But she couldn't keep her eyes from darting back to the desserts. Her gaze collided with Ben's, and for an instant the scene seemed to freeze. All the people happily loading their plates seemed to fade into the background. She heard none of their laughing chatter—only the heavy thud of her heart and the breath that she had to squeeze through her struggling lungs. While everything else dissolved in a kind of haze, Ben seemed to stand out from the background with painful clarity. There were grass stains on his khaki shorts and on his legs where he'd been kneeling to start the hibachis. The black knit shirt he wore stretched tightly across his shoulders. Above it, his face was still deeply tanned, though not quite as bronzed as Paula remembered from their first meeting. His lean brown cheeks were a sharp contrast to his blue eyes and his silvery mane of waving hair.

Then he turned away and everything slid back into focus. "I'd like to try a piece of that cake," she heard him tell Nat. "How about cutting me a big slice?"

Picking up her plastic fork, Paula nervously rearranged some of the salad still left on her plate. It would make things so much easier if she could leave now and go home, but the picnic was really only just beginning. There would be games of volleyball and badminton. The adults, who rarely saw each other during the rest of the year, would sit together in their folding lawn chairs and gossip. She would be considered unneighborly if she didn't stick around.

Small talk had never been one of Paula's talents. In the past when someone had brought out the inevitable frisbee to toss back and forth, she had gladly joined in. But since the frisbee players this year were Ben, Liz, Katy and Bob, she hung back with the older people on the street. She made herself chat about the lack of success of her vegetable garden and the oppressive heat they'd all suffered through during the summer. She commiserated about the awesome gas and electric bills and joined everyone in the hope that the fall would be pleasant and the winter not too bad.

But all the while she surreptitiously watched Ben and Liz and struggled with knife-edged pangs of jealousy. It was a relief when the sun finally began to slip over the horizon and she could decently excuse herself. But when Paula had carried her empty cake plate back into her kitchen and set it on the counter, she stood staring down at it for a long time, her shoulders slumped.

There was a confused, hollow feeling in her stomach. She tried to dismiss it but couldn't. When she'd left the picnic, Ben and Liz had been playing a spirited game of badminton. Several people had commented on what an attractive couple they'd made, and she'd had to agree. They seemed so well suited to each other and to be having such a good time together. "Well," Paula muttered aloud, "if that doesn't end any speculation about him and me, nothing will."

But the thought didn't cheer her up. There were a few dabs of cake left on the empty platter. Paula reached out a finger and brought a bit of frosting to her lips. It was dark and rich and sweet. Had it tasted as good to Ben when he'd sampled it?

Sighing, she began to walk toward the hall.

"Hey, Mom!" Nat called. He poked his head in the side door. "Ben is getting together a game of touch football. Don't you want to watch?"

"No," Paula returned wearily. "I'm feeling a little tired. I think I'll lie down for a while."

BEN WATCHED as Liz Mannion backed out of his driveway and then headed her spruce-green Volvo sedan out to the street. When she was gone he heaved a sigh of relief and walked back to his empty house. Liz was a great gal, but he preferred her in small doses. This afternoon had been just exactly long enough. Before closing the front door behind him, he turned and glanced down toward the end of the cul-de-sac. The picnic had been over for a couple of hours. Katy and her new young man had already gone back to Washington. So once again, he was all alone.

It was beginning to be the story of his life, Ben thought as he fished a cold beer out of the refrigerator, grabbed the unread stack of mail on the counter and took it all with him to the patio. Funny, he'd been looking forward to this picnic all week—thinking that he'd see Paula there and maybe get a chance to say a few words. But they hadn't exchanged a syllable.

She'd looked beautiful with that dress clinging to her lissome body and floating around her legs. He'd never seen her hair done like that before. It had suited her, emphasizing the purity of her clean, regular features, but it had also made her seem even more remote and unapproachable.

Several times he'd been sorely tempted to walk up and speak to her. But knowing how sensitive she was about gossip, he'd refrained. Actually that had been one of the reasons he'd invited Liz Mannion. He'd figured that being seen with another woman would lay some of the tattle to rest.

Another reason was that he'd wanted an ally, someone to talk to if Paula gave him the cold shoulder. He and Liz went way back, and she'd come through for him, just the way he'd known she would. Sighing, Ben snapped the tab on his beer and took a long swallow. Why couldn't he have fallen in love with a sensible woman like Liz instead of a mixed-up blonde who was tied up in knots about her "image"? But he knew the answer. Liz was a perpetual motion machine. She'd never turned him on. But all he had to do was think about Paula Kirk's quiet beauty and his blood began to boil.

Sighing once more, he began to sort through his mail. It was mostly bills and advertising. There as one circular, however, that caught his eye. It was a brochure from the recreation department that had been mailed to all county residents. Ben opened it and began to read through the offerings.

It was easy to see Paula's hand in the document, which was in many ways very impressive. It included offerings for just about everyone: fitness and sports programs for adults, classes in ballet, tap and jazz for children, intramural leagues, parent-child swimming classes. There were courses in cooking and crafts for seniors, a variety of activities designed for teens and, of course, there was Paula's pet project, the wilderness program. It featured backpacking adventures, bicycle excursions, canoe trips and hikes.

After he'd browsed through the lengthy circular, Ben closed it and looked thoughtfully at the attractive drawing of an autumn leaf on its cover. Paula would be leading a lot of those outdoor events. With a hollow ache he pictured how she'd looked on the river splash in her shorts and with her golden hair in a long braid down her back. To go hiking in the fall, she'd probably wear jeans. Come to think of it, he'd never seen her in jeans. He'd bet his last dollar that she looked damn good in them. He took another swallow of beer. There were so many things they had yet to discover about each other. The ache became raw. Why was she shutting him out, he asked himself yet again. What in hell was wrong?

Restlessly he got up and stood looking around the yard. The days were getting shorter, and night had long ago fallen. He should go in. There was a pile of work on his desk that needed to be done, and of course, Phil Walcutt wanted a decision on this election in San Cristo. Ben rubbed his thumb along the crease in his brow. He owed Phil a favor. But right now he didn't feel like making difficult decisions. Maybe taking a run in the woods would settle him down, he told himself.

Quickly he donned shorts and sneakers and then headed out to the street at a steady lope. Over the past few weeks he'd devised a route for himself that he calculated was roughly four miles long. Following his route meant running on the street for most of the way, but the last leg was on the pathway system that wound through the wooded stream valley behind Parcel Court. By the time he reached that section, he'd settled down to a tireless, long-legged stride.

Ben enjoyed running at night. There was a certain risk of course. The path was badly rutted in places, so he had to watch where he was going if he didn't want to twist an ankle. It was quite clear out, though. The slice of moon pinned to the sky was bright enough to see by.

Just then Ben became aware that he was not the only runner in the valley. Someone up ahead was setting a pace almost as steady as his own. Ben rounded a curve and caught a pale flash through the screen of trees. His eyes narrowed. Maybe he was hallucinating, but he thought that whoever was running up there had a lot of light-colored hair. Could it be Paula? To his knowledge, she was not in the habit of running at night. But she did jog. His heart beating a little faster, he lengthened his stride.

IT WAS CRAZY to be out at this hour, Paula thought as she thudded along the moon-streaked path. But she'd felt so jittery earlier, and she'd known she hadn't a hope of getting to sleep. Finally she'd thrown her customary caution aside, donned shorts and jogging shoes and told herself that if any muggers were hanging out in the woods, she'd probably be able to outdistance them.

It felt good to be running under the moon. The path was a beckoning silver track, with the creek a parallel strip of gleaming tinsel. The tall trees seemed both alien and sheltering, their furred masses mysterious dark shapes against the star-bright sky. Paula hadn't bothered to tie her hair back. It hung loose, bouncing a pleasant tattoo against her shoulder blades as she flew along the wooded passageway. Here in the shifting darkness there was a glorious sense of isolation as well as freedom. She took deep breaths, inhaling in the damp, leafy ambience and listening to the sounds of the night. One could almost forget one's problems down here, she thought. Almost.

Then suddenly she became conscious that she was not alone. The back of her neck tingled. Someone was following. Probably just another runner, she told herself with an unreasonable twinge of resentment. Not caring to have her privacy intruded upon by anyone, she increased her pace. But she quickly realized that the person behind her was coming up very fast, almost as if he were deliberately pursuing her. The thought sent a small shaft of alarm through Paula's body. Actually, she was not far from the spot where the path gave access to Parcel Court. It couldn't be more than an eighth of a mile from here.

She began to press harder, running fast enough now that her hair streamed out behind her in a pale, windborn cloud. Her heart was beating furiously, pumping blood to every nerve and cell. Adrenaline spurted through her system, making her feel strong and fleet. Some primal instinct decreed that she should not be caught.

Despite all this, Paula sensed that her pursuer was rapidly closing the distance between them. She glanced over her shoulder and caught a glimpse of a shadowy shape through the trees—a man following with the tireless, terrifying determination of a predator running down its quarry. Panic shot through her. Just over the bridge and then it wouldn't be more than fifty yards to a place where she could exit the path. Her feet pounded a frantic staccato. Her elbows were pressed close to her side and her chest forward as she gasped for air. She thought she heard her name called. Ignoring it, she ran for the bridge.

But the place where the structure met the asphalt was uneven. She caught the tip of her canvas shoe on a loose board and was sent sprawling headlong.

10

"PAULA, FOR GOD'S SAKE! Are you all right?"

She moaned a faint protest as strong hands took her by the shoulders and pulled her into a sitting position.

"Why wouldn't you stop? Didn't you know it was me?"

"No, how could I know? You frightened me." But she had known, she realized. Something within her had sensed that her pursuer was Ben. Paula leaned forward and rubbed her ankle. It felt like it might be twisted.

"You've got a nasty scrape on your knee. Do you want me to help you up?"

Propping her perspiring forehead against the heel of her hand, she shook her head. "No, I just want to sit here for a couple of minutes."

Ben squatted down, his gaze fixed on the hair that had spilled around her face and shoulders. Moonlight drenched it, giving it an unearthly sheen.

"You're damn fast when you want to be," he commented wryly.

"In high school I ran sprints on the track team."

Restraining the impulse to reach out and touch her, he swallowed and looked up at the moon. "Paula, this can't go on. We have to talk."

"Yes," she agreed. Her face was still hidden by her streaming hair.

In pure bafflement, Ben contemplated her. "Today at that picnic you behaved as if I were nothing to you."

"You didn't speak to me, either. You were too busy laughing with that brunette," she snapped back.

He absorbed the injured tone of her voice and was even more confounded. "Paula, Liz and I are only friends."

"Very good friends."

"Yes, very good friends. We've known each other for years, but I've never been her lover, if that's what you're thinking. Now that I've met you, there's not a chance that I ever will be."

She lifted her eyes, and he saw that they were huge and wet. He didn't know if tears were about to spill from them because she'd hurt herself or because of the situation between them. He only knew that he wanted to kiss away her unhappiness and hold her tight. When he spoke next his voice was rough with repressed emotion.

"Dammit, Paula, I think you were jealous this afternoon. All right, maybe I brought Liz because I hoped you would be. But if you care enough about me to be jealous, why are you trying to drive me away?" He stared as if he were trying to see into her head. "You care for me. I know you do. You wouldn't have allowed me to become your lover otherwise."

She gave a barely perceptible nod. "No."

"You're not the type for a casual affair. You need commitment, a settled way of life. I want to give you those things."

Ignoring the tears that were now tracking her cheeks, she looked at him through the darkness. "Do you really think you can? You *are* the type for a casual affair, and you don't need commitment."

"Correction. I was that way once. I've already admitted it. But it's not the case now. Paula, let's put an end to all this nonsense. Let's come out in the open about our relationship. Marry me. Be my wife."

"You've already tried marriage and found it wasn't to your taste." Her arms circled her scraped knees and huddled them against her chest.

It was like talking to a recorded message, he thought. He just wasn't getting through. Annoyed and frustrated because she wasn't giving him a chance, Ben raked a hand through his sweat-dampened hair. "I've changed. I moved here with the idea of making a new life for myself. I want a wife, a home, companionship, stability. All those things I gave up on before are necessary to me now." Firmly he put his hand under her chin and tipped her face up to his. "Paula, why won't you understand? I've fallen in love with you. I want to make a life with you."

She stared. "You've fallen in love with me?"

"Yes. I don't know when exactly. I think almost from the start—certainly after the first night we spent together."

"Oh, Ben . . ."

"You love me, too. I know it even if you don't."

"Love is such a big word. I'm confused. I don't know what I feel."

"Then marry me and we'll sort it out afterward."

"Ben, I just . . . I just can't be so casual about it!" It was an anguished cry.

"What have you got against marriage? You've told me that your first one was happy."

"Yes, but I'm not the person I was then. You say you've changed—well, so have I. I have a career... interests.... I'm not willing to devote my entire life to cooking and cleaning and running a house."

Ben rocked back on his heels. "Who asked you to do anything like that? I can cook my own meals and pay for maid service. Is that what this is all about? I'm begging you to be my wife because I want to build a future with you, not chain you to a food processor."

"Marriage is a big decision. We don't really know each other. A few stolen hours together—that's not really knowing each other...." Refusing to look at him, she pulled away from his hand and struggled to stand up. Grimly he surged to his feet and then dragged her upright and stared down into her face.

"If you want to put it like that, maybe the only way to really get to know a person is to live with them. You're not going to cohabit with me in any other fashion, so I'm willing to take a chance on marriage. Why won't you meet me halfway?"

"There's Nat—"

"He doesn't dislike me. He'll adjust."

Pulling away, she tested her weight on her sore ankle and then took a faltering step. "I don't even know what you do for a living. But I do know it's more than just running that pet shop."

"All right." He matched her steps as she began to hobble in the direction of Parcel Court. "The pet shop is just a sideline, something I'm doing primarily for fun. I have income from investments and I do a kind of consulting for the government. That's all I can say right now, but later on I can tell you more."

She choked back an unhappy laugh. "And you expect me to commit my life to yours on the basis of that? Tell me something, is this consulting you do ever dangerous?" She waited for an answer. When it didn't come, she shot him a quick, comprehending glance. "It is, isn't it?"

"Paula, I can't answer."

"You can't answer a question like that? What do you expect me to think?"

"I expect you to trust me."

"You make it sound so simple, and maybe for you it is. But for me, that's not true. Marriage is a much more total commitment for a woman than it is for a man."

"I dispute that."

"You can dispute it all you want. I know because I've been through it."

"Through what?" He moved to confront her. "You've been so closemouthed about your marriage to Tim Kirk that I don't really know anything about your life with him. The kind of arrangement I have in mind would be an equal partnership." Even standing still, she was wobbling and he took an elbow to steady her.

"Ben, I do care for you. I do. But I'm just not ready yet for a commitment like marriage. It's too soon." She looked up at him, her eyes pleading. "Can't you understand that? You once told me your first marriage failed because the timing wasn't right for you. Well, it's not right for me."

Ben's gaze narrowed. "Paula, your husband's illness must have been a hellish experience. Are you afraid you might have to go through the same thing with me?"

"Of course not."

"I'm not so sure. Sometimes I think there's a lot going on inside you that even you don't understand. Well, in case you're wondering, I'm as healthy as a horse."

"Tim would have said that about himself," she shot back. "It wasn't true."

There was a brief flash of enlightenment in Ben's mind. "That's it, isn't it? All this talk about your career and your not wanting to be a housewife—that's just a smoke screen. What you're really afraid of is that, by loving me and accepting me as a permanent part of your life, you'll be leaving yourself open to getting hurt again."

Paula was beginning to lose her temper. She was tired and emotionally overwrought. Her sore ankle and scraped knees hurt. Now Ben was pushing her unmercifully, not giving her a chance. Stubbornly she kept her head down and refused to answer him. She stumbled along for several more yards while he continued to match steps with her. Then, with a grunt of annoyance, he bent and hoisted her into his arms.

When she realized what he was doing, she started to sputter.

"Be still," he hissed.

"I don't want you to carry me."

"I'm doing it anyway." In charged silence, he bore her the rest of the way to her driveway and up its slope to her front door, and she couldn't help remembering how he'd tenderly carried her during the river splash. There were a lot of parallels between that time and this, but the emotions were painfully different. Wordlessly he deposited her on her feet.

"Ben, I—"

"Not another word. I don't want to hear another word! You say the time isn't right for you. Well, I haven't got any more time." He kissed her with a fierce pressure that was a brand rather than a caress and then strode off without looking back.

EVEN IF IT HADN'T BEEN for her swollen ankle, Paula wouldn't have tried to calm her jittery nerves by going running after dark again. Instead, when she couldn't sleep, which was almost every night, she moved a chair next to her bedroom window and spent the restless evenings staring out at the darkness and trying to think. *What am I going to do?* she asked herself. But she couldn't seem to find an answer. Where Ben was concerned, she couldn't seem to think straight at all.

Two days after her confrontation with him, there was a violent electrical storm. As Paula sat listening to the boom of thunder and watching jagged streaks of energy crack open the sky, she remembered what he'd once told her about pouring himself a glass of brandy and looking out at the lightning while he thought of her. At the time she believed he was merely flirting. Now, instinctively, she knew it must have been true.

Was she on his mind now the way he was on hers? No matter what she did or where she went, she seemed to carry Ben's lean image with her. And that, she acknowledged, was because she loved him. How could she continue to deceive herself? She wanted to be with him all the time, longed for his touch, the sound of his voice. She was in love with him—madly, totally, to the point of utter absurdity. But marriage?

They were so different in so very many ways. She had a safe, predictable life-style, and he had a mysterious background and even more inscrutable present. An affair was one thing. But marriage? How could such an alliance between them ever work?

Paula sat gazing out her window, trying to make sense of her feelings. As she examined the things she'd said and done, her actions didn't seem particularly rational. Her dread of Bernadette Carstairs's gossip, for instance. Was it reasonable to allow something so trivial to ruin a relationship with a man she now acknowledged that she loved? Or had she been using that as an excuse to push Ben away because she was afraid of what he offered?

"Smoke screen," he'd called it. Maybe he was right. After Tim's death, she'd been emotionally burned out. She'd never wanted to be threatened by life again. She'd only wanted to be safe. Living with a man like Ben Gallagher would be exciting but never safe.

Though the night was warm, Paula shivered and drew her light cotton robe tightly around her shoulders. What were the alternatives, she asked herself. Across the street, Bernadette Carstairs's big house was as dark as a tomb. Paula's eyes narrowed as she recalled what Bob had said about Bernadette. At the picnic, Katy's friend had hit the nail on the head. Vicious though she sometimes seemed, the neighborhood gossip was actually a pathetic woman. She harassed others, trying to make their lives miserable in a myriad of petty ways, because her own existence was so empty and unsatisfying. Years ago, she'd shut herself up in her house, preferring to dwell on her disappointments rather than take any more risks and try to make something positive out of her life.

"Is there any chance that I'll eventually wind up just like her?" Paula muttered into the darkness. It was a horrifying speculation, and again she shivered.

A WEEK INTO SEPTEMBER, the weather changed dramatically. With temperatures sliding to the comfortable seventies, Paula was inspired to wash some sweaters. When Nat came home from school, he found her spreading damp bundles out on towels in the backyard. Nat wrinkled his nose. "That stinks."

"They'll probably never bottle the aroma of wet wool and sell it for perfume," his mother agreed.

"Yuck! I'm going to get out of here till that smell goes away. I'm going up to Martin Square to get fish food," he informed her cheerfully.

Paula sat back on her heels. "Oh?" Six days had crawled past since she'd laid eyes on Ben. She cleared her throat. "Say hello to Mr. Gallagher for me."

"Oh, he won't be there. It'll just be Lou minding the store."

She turned her head. "Why won't Mr. Gallagher be there?"

"He's gone away."

"Gone away where?"

"I don't know—just away. He hasn't been around all week."

She shaded her eyes against the sun, partly to hide the anxious look she suspected had come into them. "Do you know when he's coming back?"

"No. It's a big mystery. Well, see ya."

After Nat had disappeared around the side of the house, Paula slipped back and sat down heavily in the grass. There was no rational reason to feel so disturbed. Ben had every right to go out of town for a few days. He'd done it several times before. Still, jabs of alarm began to poke at her insides. What if he were going out of town because he was making arrangements to sell the pet shop and move on? She'd always known that he was a rolling stone. Certainly she hadn't given him a reason to try being anything else. Or what if he'd gone away because of something dangerous connected with his job?

The sun was beating down on her head, and her temples were starting to throb. Once again, Paula put a hand up to her forehead. For three days she'd been trying to get up the courage to walk across the street and knock on the door. It was disturbing to learn that, even if she'd done so, he would have been long gone. In fact, he must have left almost immediately after that night on the path. Had he decided to look for something and someone else to fill the void in his life? She remembered his remark about not having any time. What had he meant by that?

"No point in getting hysterical," she told herself sternly. It wasn't as if Ben hadn't disappeared before and come back within a day or two. She knew he'd already paid six months rent on his house, but if he did do a vanishing act and leave without saying goodbye, whose fault was it? She knew she had only herself to blame.

For the next ten days Paula kept a close watch on Ben's house. *I'm turning into another Bernadette already*, she thought as she peered out her bedroom window. She kept hoping to see his BMW pull into the driveway, but the house on the corner just stared back at her indifferently. Once, she did catch sight of a male figure mowing Ben's lawn. Her heart had almost jumped out of her throat. A second look had told her it wasn't Ben. When she'd ventured over to investigate, it had turned out to be Jerry Sarno, a teenager who lived a couple of blocks away. He'd been hired to keep the place trim, and had no idea when his employer would be coming back.

The same was true of Lou Daniels, Ben's assistant at the shop. Swallowing the last shreds of her pride, Paula had gone there to see what she could learn, but Lou hadn't been any more informative than Jerry or Nat.

"I don't know when Mr. Gallagher is coming back," he'd told her with a shrug. "He said it could be several weeks."

As she recalled this disappointing conversation with Lou, Paula sighed heavily and started to turn from the window. Then a flash of color caught her eye and she swiveled back, her heart leaping with ridiculous excitement. There was a car pulling into Ben's drive. But it wasn't a blue BMW; it was a little silver Honda. A moment later, she saw a familiar figure climb out from behind the wheel.

"Katy," Paula breathed. If anyone knew where Ben had gone, surely it would be his daughter.

Shamelessly, Paula clattered down the stairs and ran out the front door. By the time Paula had jogged across the street, the petite redhead had let herself into her father's house. Paula rang the doorbell and stood fidgeting on the porch until Katy reappeared.

The girl's friendly face split into a wide grin. "Hi there."

"Hi yourself." Paula managed an answering smile. "Do you mind if I come in? I'd like to talk to you a minute."

"Of course not." Katy opened the screen door and then stood aside. "I just got here myself. Dad asked me to pick up his mail and see if any bills need paying. Oh, yes—" she made a little face "—and feed his fish. How about a cup of coffee? I was just about to fix myself one."

Paula followed her to the kitchen, which had an unused, faintly musty feeling about it. Katy quickly mended that. After setting water to boil on the stove, she threw open the window. The fresh air and her sunny personality made the place instantly more cheerful.

"Listen, while you sort through your father's mail, I'll feed his fish if you like."

"Oh, would you?" Katy looked grateful. "I'll show you where they are. There are instructions pasted on each tank."

Paula didn't need to be shown where to find Ben's fish tanks, but she allowed Katy to lead her down the hall and point out the rooms where they were kept. When the girl left her alone, she gazed around at the silent aquariums. Romeo and Juliet, the two discus she'd admired so many weeks ago when she'd first met Ben, stared back at her mournfully.

"You miss him, too, don't you?" she whispered as she glanced at the instructions and then picked up their box of fish food.

A few minutes later Paula returned to the kitchen and sat down at the table. "How's school coming along?"

"Great." Katy bustled about getting mugs loaded with instant coffee. "Did Dad tell you I'm following in his footsteps? I'm majoring in international relations, with a minor in languages."

"I think he mentioned that. How's your friend Bob?"

"He's great, too." She poured boiling water into the mugs and carried them to the table. "Sometimes he can be so stuffy. But, still, he's a dear." She winked. "He doesn't even realize it half the time, but he keeps me up to date on all the latest gossip at the National Protection Agency." Katy's grin was pure mischief. "Little ole Katy Gallagher has her finger on the pulse of the nation's security."

Paula laughed but then sobered as she came to her next, not very subtle query. "And your father? I haven't seen him around lately. How's he?"

Katy's grin slipped. "That's something I wish I knew the answer to myself."

"What do you mean?" Paula couldn't keep the anxiety out of her voice, but the younger woman didn't seem to hear it. Absentmindedly Katy stirred her coffee and puckered her brow.

"You know how things are around this place. Everything's a big secret. But when Dad went away, I badgered Bob until he found out what was going on. Dad's on another one of his missions."

"Mission!" Paula stared. "You don't mean he's gone off to South America again, do you?"

Katy's pretty mouth turned down. "'Fraid so."

"But . . . but I thought he'd given up that sort of life."

"I thought so, too. He swore up and down that he was never going to do it again." Clearly unhappy, Katy tugged at one of her curls. "But I guess Mom was right. You can't teach an old dog new tricks and a leopard can't change its spots and all that garbage." She sighed. "I just pray that his luck holds and he gets out alive again this time."

"Alive!" Paula was aghast. "What do you mean? Where is he? What's he doing?" The questions tumbled over each other.

"According to Bob, Dad's in San Cristo."

"San Cristo? What's he doing there?"

"Something pretty darned dangerous!"

Paula stared at her young informant, but she wasn't really seeing her. Instead, she was trying to remember everything she knew about San Cristo. It was one of those small Central American trouble spots that seemed to be in a constant state of revolution. Its recent history had been particularly brutal—kidnappings and assassinations of major political figures, bombings, bloody fighting in the street.

"He's been sent there at the request of San Cristo's government," Katy continued. "They want him to supervise the installation of the computerized voting system for the national election. I'm worried sick because I know the counterrevolutionaries have threatened to kill any American advisors who try to insure the legitimacy of that election."

The last vestiges of color drained from Paula's face. "My God," she muttered, "why did he go?"

"I wish I knew," Katy answered. "I just can't figure him out. It's true he's seemed kind of depressed the last couple of weeks, but before that, I was sure he was happy with the start he was making here. He was tired of his old life. I could feel it. And he was so darn positive about wanting to change things and settle down." Katy took a sip of her coffee. "It just doesn't make sense."

But it did. To Paula, there was a horrible logic to it—one that made her knees tremble and her stomach shrivel with anguish.

"Are you all right?" Katy asked. "You look awfully pale all of a sudden. Can I get you something?"

"No," Paula answered, totally unable to wipe the stricken look from her eyes. "But I think I'd better go home now. Thanks, Katy. Thanks for telling me."

"Sure." The girl stared after Paula as she stumbled from the kitchen. Then comprehension began to dawn on Katy's pert, freckled face. "Paula," she called, "wait!" Jumping to her feet, she rushed across the room and squeezed the older woman's hand. "Dad's pretty tough, and he knows how to take care of himself. He'll come back."

Though she appreciated the girl's kindness, the assurance seemed to roll off Paula's back. She knew that she'd given herself away completely, but she didn't care. So what if Katy realized that her father had made another conquest? Nothing seemed to matter now.

Once she was back across the street in her own house, Paula sank into the couch in front of the television set. She felt sick. Her skin was cold to the touch and her hands were trembling. Why had Ben done this? Had he known he would be going to San Cristo when he'd proposed marriage? Would he have let her accept without telling her that he was about to risk his life? She shook her head. Surely not. That would have been so terribly unfair, and Ben, even though he'd never been entirely open, had never been anything but honest.

"I do a kind of consulting for the government," he'd told her that night on the path. Well, now she knew what kind. He must have known then, she speculated.

Or had he decided to accept the assignment immediately after she'd refused him for the second time? It was a terrible thought. Pushing it away, she dropped her forehead to her hands and sat with her head bowed and her face hidden. This shouldn't come as such a shock, she told herself. After all, she'd had her suspicions. She'd seen that Spanish document in his desk and picked out the words *El Ejercito de los Puños*. Those were the counterrevolutionaries responsible for the death threats, of course.

Paula took a deep, shuddering breath and then tried to pull herself together. Any minute now Nat would be coming home from school. She couldn't let him find her like this. And maybe she was overreacting, she told herself hopefully. Maybe what Ben was doing wasn't as dangerous as Katy thought. He must know his job, after all.

Clinging to that notion, Paula managed to get through the rest of the afternoon. Glancing at the kitchen clock from time to time, she fixed Nat's favorite dinner early. As soon as he'd wolfed down the spaghetti and meatballs on his plate, he disappeared out the door to go bike riding with one his pals. When he was gone Paula walked to the television set and switched on the evening news.

Tensely she waited while the commentator waded through a grocery list of international catastrophes—canceled peace talks in Geneva, a downed jetliner in the Indian Ocean, turmoil in the Middle East, drought and famine in Africa.

"And in our own backyard," he continued, "there are further reports of strife in San Cristo."

Stiffening, Paula leaned forward. The image on the screen switched to a news clip showing a large, official-looking building whose outer walls were partially destroyed. Soldiers wielding submachine guns stood at menacing attention in front of the blackened rubble.

"Today the American embassy in San Cristo was assaulted by a car bomb loaded with over sixty pounds of explosives," the announcer intoned. "Though damage to the structure was significant, luckily no one was seriously injured."

As she laced her fingers together so tightly that they went white, Paula's eyes widened. Was Ben staying in the embassy? Could he have been injured by the explosion?

"The attack was one in a series aimed at sabotaging the legitimacy of the upcoming elections. As Tuesday, September 18, the date set for the elections in this tiny but tragedy-torn country draws near, fear and tension mounts," the newscaster continued. The film changed to scenes of firebombings and street battles. The technicolor horror made Paula flinch.

"The Puños, the violent counterrevolutionaries who have been fighting a grim battle to regain power, have publicly declared that the junta's attempt to establish equilibrium in the country by holding peaceful elections is doomed to failure. They threaten to assassinate the candidate who wins and promise heavy reprisals against American advisors sent here to install the election machinery and guarantee the fairness of the balloting."

Smoothly the anchorman switched to his next story, which was about a banking scandal. Paula didn't hear a word he said. Her gaze remained fixed on the television screen, where videotapes showing frantic activity on the New York stock exchange were now being flashed. But she was still seeing the bombed outer walls of the American embassy. Where had Ben been when that vehicle carrying its load of death came crashing through? The announcer had said that no one was seriously hurt. But that was sheer good fortune. In such situations, luck had a way of running out, and there were five days—five days!—left before the election in San Cristo would be held and the danger for the Americans involved would be finally over.

Paula started to shiver. The years during Tim's long illness had been terrible, but at least she'd been able to do something—offer him love and encouragement, be as helpful as possible with his physical needs. Now, though panic was spiraling inside her, there was no action she could take. Ben was in terrible danger, and she was totally helpless. All she could do was wait.

"Mom," Nat called as he walked in through the front door. "My bike has a flat. I need a new tire."

"Oh."

"Yeah." He stared at her curiously, "What's wrong with you?"

"What do you mean?"

"I don't know. You look funny—like you'd seen a ghost or something."

11

FROM BITTER EXPERIENCE, Paula knew about the agony of waiting. During Tim's illness, she'd waited and hoped, and that had been for two long, painful years. But over the next few days she discovered there were new lessons to be learned.

Each day, with her heart in her mouth, she opened the morning paper and scanned the headlines. Then, her stomach still fluttering, she read each syllable written about San Cristo. Reports of threats and violence continued, but none of the stories from the beleaguered country involved Americans. After she'd found no mention of Ben in the newspapers, Paula could then manage to get through the day. Evenings were a different story. The hour before the six o'clock news was excruciating torture. When the hands on the kitchen clock stretched vertically, she turned the television on with icy fingers and then, hardly daring to breathe, sat waiting.

There was almost always something about San Cristo—shots of street fights, a government official who'd been kidnapped, more attacks on the embassy—but, thank God, so far nothing about a man named Ben Gallagher. One night, after sitting up to watch the late report and hearing nothing new, Paula surprised herself by getting out one of Tim's tapes and

running it on the VCR. It was startling to see him looking dapper and authoritative. As she sat watching her
dead husband discoursing on events that were now
history, slow tears veiled her eyes.

Until now she hadn't been able to bear looking at any
of these old tapes. She was really saving them for Nat.
It was bittersweet to sit here listening to Tim and
watching him. It was like having the past rise up and
beckon to her. A year ago she would have answered
with all her heart. Now she couldn't do that. The present was too strong, too vital. Ben was her present and
that was where her emotions were now invested. She
put the tape away and sat staring at the blank screen.

As the eighteenth crept closer, Paula's anxiety bal-
looned. The night before the election was scheduled to
take place, she switched on the set with a feeling of
dread. It didn't take much to figure out that if the Puños
were going to sabotage the polling, they would have to
move in the next few hours. After the screen flickered
on, she hunched over it with her breath coming out in
short, nervous gasps.

San Cristo was the lead story.

"Several strategically located polling booths were
firebombed today," the announcer intoned. "Even more
disturbing—Puño bandits attempted to gun down an
American official who is in San Cristo to oversee the
smooth running of tomorrow's balloting."

An ugly picture of flames shooting out a storefront
seemed to blaze from the television. Then another image showed a lean, silver-haired man falling to the
ground in front of the same building. He rolled eva-
sively, and then leaping to his feet, he dashed for the
shelter of a parked car. All the while bullets from a

sniper in a nearby building rained down on the moving target he made, sending up little puffs of dust.

Paula's hand went to her mouth and her stomach lurched. It was Ben.

As if the horrifying footage just shown were of little consequence, the newscaster switched smoothly to a story about the efforts San Cristo's junta were making to insure the safety of voters on the morrow. There was nothing more about the assassination attempt and no word as to whether Ben had been hit by any of those flying bullets.

Frantically Paula switched from channel to channel. But there was nothing more to be learned. It was like receiving a telegraph that began "We regret to inform you," with the rest of the words too blurred to make out.

She was still standing in front of the television set wringing her hands when the phone rang. It was a moment or two before the sound penetrated her distress. When she finally picked up the receiver, her mother's voice came at her like a cat with its claws out.

"Was that Ben Gallagher I just saw on television?"

"Yes." Paula's reply was a mere whisper.

"What is that man doing, allowing himself to get shot at in a place most decent people never heard of before?"

"I don't know." Her eyes wet with tears, she stared blindly around the room. "It's his job, I think. He works for the National Protection Agency." Paula's voice broke on the last word. "Oh, Mother, I'm so worried!" she cried. "I love him and I sent him away! I never even told him how I feel. What if he never comes back? What if he's killed?"

Lynn tried to be comforting, but what could she say that would really help? The best she could do was to offer to take Nat for the next couple of days. Gratefully Paula accepted. It was going to be hard enough to get through the hours ahead without having to endure the strain of pretending, for Nat's sake, that nothing was wrong.

The next day Paula begged off going into work. There was no way she could function at the office. But staying home and pacing the floor of her family room wasn't going to accomplish anything, either. After she read every word about San Cristo in the morning papers and again found no mention of Ben, she packed a light lunch for herself, got into her car and headed north toward Weaverton. There was a state park in the scenic area, and she'd led many hikes through it. The park boasted one of her favorite sections of the Appalachian Trail and a magnificent rocky overlook. From it, one could gaze down into the deep gorge cut by the Shenandoah River and admire the surrounding foothills and mountains.

The overlook was one of nature's special places, and now Paula was drawn to it in the same way an unhappy acolyte might be attracted to an empty cathedral. The times when she'd perched on those rocks and looked out at the world spread before her had been spiritually uplifting. She needed somewhere to sort through her jumbled thoughts and emotions and to gather her strength for this new ordeal she was having to endure.

At the state park she left her car in the lot and strapped on her day pack. Reaching the overlook would take three hours of difficult hiking. But Paula looked forward to the exercise. Her troubled spirit craved the distraction of hard, physical effort. She set off briskly on the uphill climb.

Much later in the afternoon, when she arrived at her destination, her jersey top was glued to her breasts by perspiration and her hair was clumped around her damp forehead. Nevertheless, it was with a sense of relief unconnected with her aching muscles that she scrambled out onto the jumbled mass of boulders. After finding a spot where she could prop her back against a jutting rock, she took a canteen out of her day pack and unwrapped a sandwich. Chewing absentmindedly on her late lunch and washing it down with occasional sips of water, she looked out over the river valley below.

Not far away, a hawk floated lazily. Beneath him, the river meandered like a flat metallic vein. All around, blue haze softened the outlines of the hills and ridges that stretched in every direction. Paula took a deep breath. Why had she never shown this spot to Ben or even mentioned it, she wondered. Of course, there hadn't been much time. But even so, she knew why there were so many pieces of herself she'd tried to keep private, why there was so much left unsaid between them.

From the moment they'd met, he'd steadily forced his way into her life, invading every one of her sanctuaries like floodwater steadily breaching a mountain of sandbags. No matter how many barriers she'd tried to build around herself, he'd knocked them flat. Finally she'd tried to contain the havoc he was wreaking on her emotions by telling herself it didn't really matter. They were merely having an affair—an affair that would soon wear itself out and leave no permanent effects.

That, she now recognized, had been a ridiculous piece of self-deception. She'd wanted to avoid commitment, the pain and risk of having one's life and deepest feelings yoked to those of another. But the deed was done. She *was* tied to Ben Gallagher. She couldn't be more terrified for his life if they were married. And if he were killed in a faraway land, her pain wouldn't be less searing because their last names were not the same.

Paula leaned her head back against the rock and closed her eyes. She loved him. A marriage ceremony would have only set the seal on something very real that already existed. "Oh, Ben," she whispered, "please come back. Don't let it end like this. Let me tell you how I feel so we can start over again."

DRIVING JUST OVER THE SPEED LIMIT, she got back to the house that evening in time for the six o'clock news. But the anchorman's election report on San Cristo only answered a few of the questions plaguing her. Though there had been several thwarted attempts to sabotage polling booths and many voters had been afraid to turn out, the elections had, on the whole, been carried out peacefully. The tiny country now had a president. Whether he would be able to stay in office remained to be seen.

About the Americans who'd risked their lives to ensure the safety and honesty of the election process there was no news. Paula could only guess when Ben would be coming home. But at least the worst was over, she told herself. For surely if he'd been murdered or seri-

ously injured, there would have been some word. Once
again she took up her vigil in front of her bedroom
window, praying that she would see his car pull into the
driveway or a light flickering somewhere in his darkened house.

Four nights later a pair of headlamps sliced through
the darkness and then were almost instantly swallowed as the driver activated a remote control door
opener and disappeared inside Ben Gallagher's garage.
Across the street, the rocker in which Paula had been
gently creaking to and fro went rigid. Her eyes un-
blinking, Paula waited for a light to appear in one of the
windows, but nothing happened. The house stayed
dark. Of course, Ben's kitchen was at the back of the
house. He could be there and from her vantage point
she wouldn't be able to tell.

On the other hand it might be Katy over there. For
several minutes Paula sat as if frozen. What should she
do? Her teeth almost chattering with the intoxicating
mixture of hope and fear that had begun to course
through her veins, she rose to her feet and rapidly paced
the length of the bedroom several times. Her heart was
thumping so fast that it felt as if it might be about to fly
out of her chest. As if she were trying to keep it from
doing that, she pressed her hand over her breast. Then
she crossed to the phone next to her bed. With fingers
that felt as brittle as dried stalks of grass, she dialed
Ben's number.

AS HE DROVE DOWN the familiar street, Ben was so tired
that he felt as if his eyes were coated with cheesecloth.
In San Cristo, sleep had been a rare commodity. Certainly he hadn't seen much. No doubt about it, his

nerves weren't what they had been. A year or two ago he would have enjoyed the high-wire tension and slept like a baby. Now being threatened and shot at produced acid in his stomach and a general feeling of distaste—as had this whole operation, including the twenty-four hour debriefing he'd just suffered through. At several points the people on Phil's staff had struck him as being more like a pack of overgrown twelve-year-olds playing cops and robbers than the hardened professionals they were.

"You're turning into an old man, Gallagher," he muttered as he swung onto Parcel Court. Briefly his gaze skated over the dark outlines of Paula's house. There were no welcome-home lights in her windows or yellow ribbons tied to the tree in her front yard, but then he hadn't expected any. Jerking his eyes away, he pulled into his driveway and then into the garage. What a homecoming, he thought as he slid wearily from behind the wheel. After the menace of the past few days, returning to Parcel Court was like stepping from a disaster movie directly into a Walt Disney production. The question was, where did he belong? Or was there anywhere he belonged anymore?

His eyes had adjusted to the dark. Not bothering to flick the switch in the hall, he wandered into the kitchen before turning on a light. The place looked deserted and smelled musty. A sinking feeling in his gut, he sat down at the kitchen table and stared at the pile of mail Katy had left. Mostly bills and advertising circulars. Why did he feel so low, he wondered. Lonely homecomings never used to affect him this way. In the old days he'd been glad to get back to an empty apartment. Not having anyone to greet him had meant he could sleep as long as he wanted without interruptions.

But that was before he'd met Paula. God, he wanted to see her so bad that it hurt. During this whole nightmarish assignment, her image had never left him. Now that he was back, it was hell to think of her being over there in that house and not being able to walk across the street and knock on her door. But she didn't want him. She'd made that quite clear. He put a hand up to push back the mop of hair that had slipped over his forehead, then let his palm rest against his aching temples a moment.

Just then he was jerked from his unhappy reverie by the buzz of the telephone. He glanced at his watch. It was almost eleven. Who could that be? But when he picked up the receiver and said hello, there was no answer. The silence on the other end of the line was as deep as the night and just as filled with hidden life.

Ben's forehead wrinkled. "Who is this?" The person who had called him wasn't saying a word, just listening and holding their breath.

Scowling, Ben hung up. In his line of business he'd made too many enemies to be amused by crank calls. He never knew who might be after him. It could be anyone from a Puño assassin to Bernadette Carstairs down the street. He laughed humorlessly and then opened a kitchen cabinet and took out a half-full bottle of Scotch. Come to think of it, given a choice, he'd take on the assassin any day.

After filling a tumbler with ice cubes he poured some of the Scotch over them and went outside to the patio. Given his exhaustion, he should really be falling into bed, but he felt too restless for that. There were too many things churning around inside him. Like, what was he going to do about Paula? That was the big question mark in his life now. Paula.

He took a sip of Scotch and looked up at the starry sky. It was a mild night, but the year was getting on. It wouldn't be long before he'd be hearing the honk of migrating geese overhead. Was that what he should be doing, picking up and taking himself elsewhere? He'd wanted to build a life here, but without Paula the attempt seemed hollow. If she didn't want him, maybe the gentlemanly thing to do was get out of her way.

"But since when have you been a gentleman, Gallagher," he muttered aloud. His mouth firmed and his jaw thrust forward aggressively. No. He wasn't ready to give up on the lady across the street yet. Not by a long shot!

"Ben?"

The tremulous feminine voice that had suddenly broken the silence made him jerk around and stare. He stood up and peered into the darkness. "Paula, is that you?"

"Yes. Oh, Ben! Ben!"

A slim white shape flew toward him, warm arms wrapped themselves around his waist, and Paula Kirk pressed her body into his. "Ben, I'm so glad to see you," she cried breathlessly. "I was so worried, so worried!" Her arms tightened and she let out a sound that was half a sob and half a cry of joy.

Paula clung to Ben and buried her face in the open collar of his shirt. When she'd heard him on the phone, she'd been in such a hurry to rush across and see him that she hadn't stopped to think about what she intended to say. Now disconnected words and phrases poured out of her. "Oh, Ben, how could you leave like that? Why didn't you tell me?" she choked out.

Dumbfounded, he stood there staring down at her as if she were an apparition. Then he gently disengaged himself and took a step back. "Paula? What's this all about?"

She pressed her hands together and gazed at him through wet eyes. Though she really couldn't see him very well because of her tears, he was still beautiful. It was so wonderful that he was standing there, apparently unharmed. She wanted to laugh and cry and smother him with kisses. Instead, she managed to quaver, "Are you really all right? I saw your car, and then when you answered the phone . . ."

"Was that you who called me just now?"

"Yes."

"My God, why didn't you say so? I was imagining all sorts of things."

She shook her head helplessly. "I don't know. I should have but I couldn't seem to. When I heard you answer, all I could think about was coming across here to see you." She looked at him yearningly. He was holding himself so aloof from her, staring at her as if he couldn't believe his eyes. Was he still angry, she wondered. She took a step toward him and laid a tentative hand on his arm. "Oh, Ben, I was so worried! Why did you leave like that? Why didn't you tell me you were going?"

"I couldn't tell you, and besides, I didn't think you'd care."

The flat statement hit her like a blow and she flinched. "Not care? Of course I care. Ben, I love you!"

The look of amazement on his face was even more painful. Had he really not known? Casting aside what was left of her pride, she gave a little cry and wrapped her arms around his waist once more. "I'm so sorry for the way we parted," she blurted against his chest. "Will you forgive me?"

Ben continued to gaze down at her. He was having trouble believing this was happening. Had Paula Kirk actually just thrown herself at him and declared her love?

"Of course I'll forgive you," he finally whispered. "I love you. And besides, there's nothing to forgive. I was pushing you too hard. I wanted you so badly that when you started to draw back, I grew desperate and grabbed like a greedy child. I should have understood that you needed time."

She shook her head. "I don't need time anymore, Ben. All I need is you."

He had to put both his arms around her, but he was still holding the tumbler of Scotch. There was no place to set it, so he tossed it into the bushes, ignoring the dull thunk it made as it rolled beneath a clump of forsythia. The moment his hands were free he enfolded Paula and held her tight.

"Did you mean what you just said?" he questioned.

"Yes. Oh Ben, yes!" She lifted her face, and he could see that she spoke the truth. The feeling was all there, shining in her beautiful eyes.

"Oh God, Paula," he groaned. Then he was holding her face between his hands, covering her forehead, her cheeks, her lips with sharp, hungry kisses. It was as if some fragile, barely maintained restraint had suddenly snapped and he was no longer in control. His feverish caresses overwhelmed her, drowned her.

"Ben, Ben, stop! I can't breathe," she panted, grasping his wrists and laughing. "You're smothering me!"

Welding her to him, he ran his hands up and down her back. "You don't know what you've just done to me, Paula. Damn, I'm trembling!" He became aware that her shoulders were bare. "And so are you. What's this thing you're wearing? It feels as if you're naked underneath it."

"I am," she managed to gasp against his chest. "It's just my nightgown. When I ran across to your house, I didn't even think about changing my clothes."

His lips quirked. "Darling, I'm flattered, but dashing around in the dark to visit a bachelor in your nightie might not be good for your reputation. What if Bernadette saw you?"

Against his chest, Paula produced a watery giggle. "You're right, but I don't care anymore. I don't care what anybody thinks or says."

"Since I was the bachelor you were running to, neither do I," he agreed in a deeper tone. His hands began to mold her body. As they cupped her buttocks and pressed her firmly to his pelvis, he could feel her full breasts flatten against his chest. The effect was unspeakably erotic, and his response was immediately obvious to them both. "You can tell what's going on with me," he whispered into her hair. "I want you."

"Yes."

"Yes, you know and you're shocked? Or yes, you want me back?" He hiked up her nightgown so that his fingers could slip beneath. A moment later she shivered as she felt them tracing a sensuous pattern high on the backs of her thighs.

"Both" was her muffled reply. "But mainly the latter."

He sucked in his breath. "You don't know what it's been like for me these last few weeks, and before I got away to San Cristo it was even worse. I would look across at your house and think about doing crazy things. Once I even considered scaling your drainpipe and climbing in through your bedroom window."

"What stopped you?"

"The drainpipe didn't look very sturdy. Fear of falling off your roof and making a damn fool of myself, I guess." His chuckle was gutteral. "But there's no roof to tumble from out here, is there?" As he spoke he led her to the chaise longue in back of them. Deftly he flipped its cushiony mattress onto the grass.

"What are you doing?"

"Making a nice flat, safe surface for the two of us. I want to hold you."

Paula's eyebrows flew up. "Out here? Like this?"

"Yes." He turned to her and in one smooth motion stripped the nightgown from her.

There was no time to comment. Suddenly she found herself stretched out on the tufted, cloth-covered mat with Ben's long, hard body coming down over hers. Against her flesh, his chest and legs and narrow hips made an exciting prison. When he began to run his hands up and down her sides, pausing on the bare skin of her hips and thighs, she wriggled.

"You aren't really planning on making love to me out here, are you?"

"Uh-huh." His mouth found her throat, and she shivered as he seemed to feed from her throbbing pulse. "If you have any serious objections, you'd better tell me about them now," he murmured.

"I've never done anything like that. It just seems so . . . so . . ."

"Sinful? Sinfully delicious." Ben chuckled. "The way of the transgressor may be hard, but it's also a lot of fun." As he spoke, he levered himself so that he could brush his lips back and forth across the tips of Paula's swelling breasts. The feathery teasing made her nipples tingle. Then, as he caught one of them between his teeth and sucked gently, she heard herself moan with delight. Suddenly there was nothing that she wanted more than to transgress with Ben.

Her hands went up to his head. When he lifted his head she found the underside of his jaw and nuzzled it. He needed a shave. His skin felt prickly against her lips and chin. But she liked the sensation. It was an added stimulus.

He reacted to her eager kisses with a rough sound deep in his chest. Then shockingly cool air rushed over her naked body as he rolled away and took his warmth with him. She reached out in protest, but he didn't respond because he was too busy struggling with the closure on his slacks.

"Whoever decided to bring back button flies should be horsewhipped," he muttered thickly as he undid the last of the tiny buttons.

Amused and frustrated, Paula asked, "Why did you buy them?"

"They were a Father's Day gift from Katy. She says they're the latest thing." He stepped free of the offending garment and kicked it to one side. His shirt and underwear quickly followed. She could see why he'd had so much trouble with the buttons on his pants. There had been quite a strain on them. When she said as much, he laughed and then almost fell on her, ravaging her lips and the inside of her mouth with his hot kisses until she was limp and breathless.

"I'll show you strain, my lady! It's cruel what you do to me. But now, with you beneath me like this . . ." He ground his hips into hers, the sensuous implication further inflaming both their loins.

Eagerly she moved against him. Her hands touched his body, reveling in its strength and promise. Her fingers foraged through his hair, explored the contours of his back and then slid over the smooth, tight marble of his buttocks. "Oh, Ben, I love you so much," she whispered.

His tongue drank in the words, and she could only shudder in mounting fervor. To give himself better access, he rolled slightly to one side. Expertly his fingers increased the thrilling intimacy between them. Relentlessly they excited her, and very soon her body seemed to dissolve under his hand. He knew that she was ready to receive his urgent invasion, and because of his pressing need, they came together quickly. Their overwrought emotions and Ben's exhaustion made their communion sweet but brief. When it was over they lay closely entwined, unwilling to part.

At last, with his weight a warm, insistent pressure against her legs and thighs and belly, Ben once again captured her face between his palms and stared down into it. "Moonlight suits you. When I thought of you in San Cristo, as I did every day and every night, it was with your hair a shimmer of silver and your face bathed in moonglow. Paula, I love you very much. But it's more than that. I need you." His lips moved along her hairline and then brushed her brow. "I need your softness and your warmth. I want to wake up and find you in my bed in the morning, and when I have to be away, I want to come home to your smile."

She smoothed back a lock of his hair. "You make marriage sound idyllic, but it's not. I don't walk around smiling all the time. Quite often you'd be coming home to my frown."

"Then I'll have the chance to try and wipe that frown away. Paula, come live with me and be my love. Marry me. Say we're going to make this a permanent arrangement."

She was silent so long that he became tense. Surely she wouldn't deny him now, he thought. But he couldn't be sure.

Finally she said, "Do you really think it would work? Ben, on television I saw you being shot at. It was—" her voice caught "—it was terrible! I couldn't live with that sort of fear."

"You won't have to."

"But your job . . ."

"What I was doing in San Cristo isn't my job anymore. Like I told you before, I'm a consultant. Going into active duty was a favor to my old boss—a special assignment. I didn't need to accept it."

She stared up at him, trying to make sense of what he was saying. "If you didn't need to travel there and risk your life, why did you?"

"That night on the path I was deciding whether or not to go. When you told me you wouldn't marry me, I felt so low that nothing seemed to matter. My boss called the next morning, and I agreed to take on the job."

Paula was horrified. "You mean that because of me you risked your life? I was afraid of something like that. Oh, Ben!"

He kissed her cry into muffled silence. "It doesn't matter," he whispered against her lips. "I'm back now and not a scratch on me. The only thing that matters now is the future—our future together. You haven't answered my question. Paula, say you'll marry me."

"If I say yes, will you stay home safe and sound with me?"

"I promise I won't go any farther than the pet store or our bedroom without your permission." His warm voice was alive with love and laughter.

"You can go a little farther than that."

"In another minute or two I intend to go all the way," he retorted, cupping a possessive hand over Paula's breast. "But only with you."

"As long as it's only with me," Paula agreed on a sigh. Then she gave herself up to his kiss.

Harlequin Temptation

COMING NEXT MONTH

ATTRACTIVE, SPACE SAVING BOOK RACK

Display your most prized novels on this handsome and sturdy book rack. The hand-rubbed walnut finish will blend into your library decor with quiet elegance, providing a practical organizer for your favorite hard-or soft-covered books.

Only $9.95

Approximately 16" x 8" when assembled

Assembles in seconds!

To order, rush your name, address and zip code, along with a check or money order for $10.70 ($9.95 plus 75¢ postage and handling) (New York residents add appropriate sales tax), payable to *Harlequin Reader Service* to:

In the U.S.

Harlequin Reader Service
Book Rack Offer
901 Fuhrmann Blvd.
P.O. Box 1325
Buffalo, NY 14269-1325

Offer not available in Canada.

BKR-1

Two exciting genres in one great promotion!

Harlequin Gothic and Regency Romance Specials!

GOTHICS—
romance and love growing
in the shadow of
impending doom . . .

REGENCIES—
lighthearted romances
set in England's Regency
period (1811-1820)

SEPTEMBER TITLES

Gothic Romance	Regency Romance
CASTLE MALICE	THE TORPID DUKE
Marilyn Ross	Pauline York
LORD OF HIGH CLIFF MANOR	THE IMPERILED HEIRESS
Irene M. Pascoe	Janice Kay Johnson
THE DEVEREAUX LEGACY	THE GRAND STYLE
Carolyn G. Hart	Leslie Reid

Be sure not to miss
these new and intriguing stories
. . . 224 pages of wonderful reading!